FLUKE

Other Works by Martin Blinder

Books
Lovers, Killers, Husbands and Wives
Children of the Holocaust (Editor)
Psychiatry in the Everyday Practice of Law
The Lucretia Borgia Cookbook
Choosing Lovers
Smart Travels

StagePlays
The Perfect Man
Profile for Murder
A Passionate Man
The Wedding Present

FLUKE

by

Martin Blinder

THE PERMANENT PRESS
SAG HARBOR, NY 11963

Library of Congress Cataloging-in-Publication Data

Blinder, Martin.
Fluke / by Martin Blinder
p. cm.
ISBN 1-57962-017-5
1. Harding, Warren G. (Warren Gamaliel) 1865-1923
Fiction. 2. Britton, Nan, B. 1896--fiction
I. Title.
PS3552.L468F58 1999
813'.54--dc21 98-27860
CIP

THE PERMANENT PRESS
4170 Noyac Road
Sag Harbor, NY 11963

For Tracey Washington and Barbara Braun:
there through thick and thin.

Acknowledgments

The author is indebted to the Harding Memorial Society, the Hoover Institute, the Library of Congress, and the Smithsonian Institute for generous access to private collections and other research materials in the preparation of this novel.

Throughout, dialogue has been created, time compressed, and minor characters combined. All significant historical and biographical events, however, are factually depicted; most are a matter of public record. Sad to say, this is a true story.

the first president to be loved by his
"bitterest enemies" is dead
the only man woman or child who wrote
a simple declarative sentence with seven grammatical
errors "is dead"
beautiful Warren Gamaliel Harding
"is" dead

e. e. cummings

I may not be the smartest President to ever sit in the White House but by God I'll be the best loved.

Warren Gamaliel Harding
President of the United States
1921—1923

PROLOGUE

San Francisco, August 24th, 1923.

Beneath a pewter sky on a misty afternoon, a presidential funeral procession inches down Market Street. The broad boulevard is lined twenty or more deep with bereaved of every age—hats in hand, tears, heads bowed, a flutter of damp handkerchiefs. Wordlessly they watch as the coffin of Warren Gamaliel Harding, draped in black crepe and resting in an uncovered carriage, rolls slowly past them pulled by four horses. Following are a half-dozen gargantuan, open limousines —Packards, La Salles, and Pierce-Arrows—bearing dignitaries and family, for whom the President's voice, rich, warm and resonant—like fine bourbon— has been forever stilled.

With so much left to say:

Being dead has its good points. The pain ends. No more insoluble problems. No more betrayals. You're well out of the turmoil, the futile struggle. Now it's all in someone else's hands. Well good riddance. To the whole damn lot. 'Cept for my sweet Nan—I sure wasn't ready to give ***her*** *up. Not in this lifetime.*

He sighs.

Nor the next.

A light breeze rustles the crepe covering the coffin.

Yup, that's me in the box. Or I suppose, what used to be me. Warren G. Harding, your twenty-ninth President. Till a few nights ago.

The procession creeps forward past mist-heavy flags hanging lifelessly at half mast. Drowsing in the Packard phaeton just behind the presidential caisson is a gaunt, dour sixty-three-year-old man in a black coat and top hat.

That there's the new fellow. Calvin Coolidge. God help America. Old Pickle-Face can fall asleep any time, anywhere.

Coolidge yawns.

Sorry if we disturbed your rest, Calvin. You get to nap in the White House all you want now.

Staring straight ahead, the late President's wife, Florence, sits stiffly alongside Coolidge. There is no discernible human connection between them—they could be at opposite ends of the earth. A veil obscures Florence's deeply lined face but can do little to soften a jutting iron jaw.

And of course, my missus. Stuck next to Pickle-Face, poor dear. Talk about a determined woman. Fact is, she would have made one heck of a stronger president than I ever was. Loved you, Duchess. The best I could. Lord knows you deserved better. Hmmph, hope she doesn't spot Nan. Where ***is*** *that child anyway?*

As the cortege lumbers past, one, then others amongst the mourners point, or tug on a neighbor's sleeve, as they recognize the smug face of Harry Daugherty, a bluff, bald, middle-aged man sitting opposite Coolidge.

Now ***there's*** *the man of the hour. Harry's a famous fellow these days in his own right. Naturally, elbowed his way into the first car.*

From time to time, Daugherty responds to his newfound celebrity with a nod, or tip of the hat.

An old and devoted friend, too, Harry Daugherty. More than anyone, it was Harry who got me to Washington. Then all through my presidency he labors quietly by my side. Your model selfless, anonymous public servant. Today that crooked puss of his is on the front page of every goddamn newspaper in the country! Jeez, was I ever blind! "Half-step Harry" they're calling him now—barely a half-step ahead of the law. Turns out the sonofabitch had his hands in every till. God Almighty, who can a man trust?

And ***where*** *the hell's Nan?*

Desolate young people are everywhere along Market Street, though apparently, none of them Nan. The procession crosses the intersection at New Montgomery. Two weeping pubescent girls toss handfuls of rose petals on the road just ahead of the caisson's wheels. Nearby, an inconsolable, elderly black man blows his nose. A small boy in a sailor suit salutes.

Will you look at all these good people! You'd think some great personage had passed on. They know so little about the mess I left. Tell ya—I had no business in that job. None. Awful place, the White House. Killed a lot tougher men than me.

And ***there's*** *another weasel who sure didn't help matters.*

Chewing on a plug of tobacco, a lanky, ruddy, mustachioed man in his sixties dominates the second car in line, an elephantine Pierce-Arrow.

Tuh! Albert Fall. Ever loyal. Salt of the earth. "Just call me Al." Always ready to lend a hand. Sure. The bastard might as well have put a gun to my head. Lemme tell ya, in Washington if you want a friend, get yourself a dog.

Fall puckers, fires a squirt of tobacco juice over the side of the car, then readjusts his derby.

Pretty jaunty for a guy hit last week with a six-count federal indictment, dont'cha think? The nerve of him—showing up here. Guess that's a problem with funerals—the fella it's all about no longer has any say. You can bet ***Henry*** *wouldn't have been invited either, had I been consulted. Ya see him— that prissy dwarf?*

Perched next to Fall is venerable Henry Cabot Lodge, an impassive, elegantly goateed, elfin man, all but engulfed by the cavernous phaeton around him.

The most bloodless, joyless, constipated fellow you'd ever want to meet. The moment Henry walks into a room it feels emptier. I'll wager he's savoring every minute of this, the skunk, though you really can't be sure—with Henry it'd be hard to distinguish grief from ecstasy. No regrets if I never see ***his*** *face again.*

But where in blazes is my precious Nan*? Gal would be late to her own funeral, but you'd think she'd at least be on time for—hey,* ***there*** *she is.*

More desolate faces as the coffin rumbles by, at last drawing parallel to a golden-haired woman at the curb, twenty-seven-year-old Nan Britton. Tears spill from her startling green eyes.

Now take a gander at that. Ever in your life see a lovelier little lady?

Nan is indeed lovely—and about five months pregnant.

Yeah, that's my bun in the oven. My very first, and—evidently—my last.

Harding's coffin passes no more than three feet in front of her—just a small step forward and Nan could touch it. Harding's voice thickens.

Ah dearest, dearest Nan Britton—the one blessing in this whole benighted world I'm really gonna miss.

Tentatively, Nan reaches out, then pulls her hand back. She gives her President a sad little wave goodbye.

President Warren Harding is remembered—if at all—as having presided over the most corrupt administration in the history of the White House.

He died in office just as the first scandals were breaking, never having had the chance to tell his side.

I know most of what went on, I think, and what he would have had to say about it, had he lived.

I loved him—and only him—almost all my life.

My name is Nan Britton, and I was his mistress.

Let me start back in a happier time, a far simpler time. . .

PART ONE

1.

Though of course, my birth certificate would maintain otherwise,so far as I am concerned, my life truly began on July 4th, 1912. Nothing in my then fifteen years on this earth could have prepared me for this crashing coming of age on that brilliant, red, white and blue morning, nor for the remarkable man who was to be its instrument.

A teenage girl's petite waving hand is but one of many sprouting from a festive, sun-drenched crowd jamming Main Street of a small, mid-American town, gathered to watch Marion, Ohio's Independence Day parade. Like last July and the several before that, the procession is led by the town's robust alderman, forty-six-year-old Warren Gamaliel Harding, astride a white stallion sashaying just ahead of a sparkling brass marching-band of uncertain pitch.

The musicians are followed by a troop of ancient, bemedaled Civil War veterans in faded Union blue, some dependent upon canes, a few pushed along in wooden wheelchairs. Next come unsmiling militants of the Anti-Saloon League, trailed by no less grim contingents of the Daughters of the American Revolution, and finally, in contrast, ebullient delegations from the Chamber of Commerce, the Ohio Grange, and the Marion Boosters Club, for all of whom next year will always be an even better one. Each troupe flourishes its own particular banners, pennants and flags as they strut along, creating a gleaming, undulating satin river of purple, gold, maroon and green. Dogs dart in and out, barking patriotically.

Alderman Harding is a boundlessly contented, classically handsome man, easily six feet, with a head you might expect on a Roman coin. He waves broadly at his townsfolk, tipping a Panama hat right and left, reveling in the heartfelt approval and affection that rises up to him all along the way.

A young man in the crowd gives Harding a mock salute. "Hullo, Alderman. Band just don't sound the same without you tootin' on that old tuba."

Harding smiles down at him. "Hey there, Greg—you back in Marion?"

"Just for the holiday. Here to see my mom."

"You tell your mom Warren Harding sends his best."

"I sure will, Warren—that'll make her real pleased."

A ruddy-faced man in overalls and a plaid shirt calls out to him. "How ya doin', Warren?"

"Doin' well, Petey. Good to see ya. Corn in yet?"

"First ears just this morning. I'll bring some by while they got all their sugar."

"Why I sure do appreciate that. Thanks, Petey."

Two young women costumed as "Miss Liberty" toss bouquets up at him. He snares them both and beams as each girl blows him a kiss. Warren Harding's contentment may be easy, but it runs the length and breadth of his soul.

The parade draws close to the fluttering teenage hand, belonging to diminutive, delicate Nan Britton, on tiptoes between her parents, bobbing up and down for a better view. Indicia of her later staggering beauty are already evident.

As a young girl I had wished desperately to grow up to be a great saint—like Joan of Arc. I would pray every night to Jesus, begging him to afflict me with some horrible disease I could suffer ecstatically, until the Pope recognized my beatific selflessness. This piety greatly alarmed my parents, neither of whom were Catholic, and most particularly, my father, who did not even believe in God. Or very much else.

Harding comes abreast of Nan, horse and rider luminous in the warm sunshine. Through the forest of bonnets, straw hats and waving American flags, she catches Harding's eye. He winks, then blinds her with his smile.

Suddenly all these aspirations for immortality vanished when, at that fateful moment, an authentic saint, a true knight on a white horse, rode into my life. In a heartbeat I'd found the man who was to forever be the center of my world. Anyone who has not experienced all-consuming devotion may well find it hard to comprehend, but Warren Harding was to touch me so deeply that I would thereafter dedicate myself to melding and blending into him, as he had inexplicably become so much a part of me.

Nan flushes. She pulls on her mother's arm and points. "Mummy, who's that?"

"Oh—that's Mr. Harding, dear. You know—the *Marion Weekly Star*? It's his little newspaper."

Nan's father frowns. "Mindless Republican rag. . . "

"How come he leads the parade, Mummy?"

"He's also everyone's favorite alderman. A *very* kind fellow. . . "

Mr. Britton grumbles loudly. "Political hack. Fawning Republican toady. . . "

Nan routinely ignores her father, having learned that however bright the sun, it has yet to shine on him. "What's an alderman, Mummy?"

"Another two-bit grafter. . . " mumbles her father.

His wife overrides him. "An alderman is—someone townsfolk vote in to sort of preside over things. Help keep Marion running along."

Mr. Britton has thoroughly warmed to the subject. "Help himself to the public trough. . . "

Nan persists. "Like they vote for the President."

"That's right, dear," affirms her mother. " 'Cept that an alderman is strictly a local official. And just part-time, I believe. Quite different from a President."

Nan's gaze remains fixed on Harding's receding figure as the parade tramps on by. "Mr. Harding looks *exactly* like I imagine a President would look."

Her father's had enough. He hits his sibilants hard, sending spittle into space. "For your information, Miss Nan, the President—William Howard Taft—is said to weigh three hundred and seventy-six pounds. The White House had to build special chairs just for him."

Nan stands her ground. "Well, Mr. Harding certainly looks much more like a President than *that*. If ladies could vote, *I'd* vote for Mr. Harding."

Nan's mother nods in vigorous agreement.

Her father shakes his head in disgust. "That's precisely why, praise heaven, ladies will never get the vote."

2.

The editorial policy of the *Marion Weekly Star* is well tailored to Harding's particular combination of strengths—a florid way with words, limited curiosity, aversion to change, and indefatigability as town booster and patriot. And reporting, as it did, only those stories which put Marion and its citizens in the best possible light, the paper is everywhere welcome, if not widely read.

Certainly one would not easily mistake the *Star* for the *Cleveland Post Dispatch*, or for that matter, the *Marion Morning Tribune*. The walls of the one-story wood frame storefront that had been its home since birth fourteen years ago were no longer plumb, if ever they were. The roof sags with fatigue. "Modest" was how Harding himself characterized his newspaper empire, always a bit behind financially and in subscribers, notwithstanding its gold letter bravado on the window:

The Marion Weekly Star
Warren G. Harding
Editor and Publisher
Paid circulation 8,750

Yet Harding tremendously enjoyed putting out his little paper, and would never consider anything else. All his life the grass always looked greener right under his feet.

Nan, in pigtails, a white pinafore and white patent leather shoes, approaches the newspaper's offices from a park across the street. She reaches the front door, then pauses to gather up her courage.

Just within, Harding and long-time United States Senator William Foraker chat politics in the front office as they savor leisurely cigars. Soft blue smoke hangs drowsily around them in the still air. The two old friends, Harding tilted back in his well-seasoned wood and leather desk chair, Foraker reclining on a battered loveseat, share in the prestigious company of Presidents McKinley, Taft, and

Theodore Roosevelt, whose framed sepia photographs eye each other from opposite walls. Harding's Airedale, Old Abe, sprawls on a frayed rug by Harding's chair, tail thumping as Harding scratches him behind the ears.

As always, Harding is reassuring. "Wouldn't think you'd have to campaign all that much this time 'round, would you, Bill? You've been down this road so many times. . . "

"Ya never know what voters will do," counters Foraker. He jabs his cigar towards Harding. "You remember that when ya make the run for Governor, Warren, my boy."

Harding laughs. "Me? I'd sooner throw myself in front of a horse. Invite all that grief. . . "

"Beware complacency," Foraker continues, "that's my motto. Look at old Blaine. Re-elected four times, figures he can rest on his laurels—and a Democrat squeaks right past him. No sir, I'm gonna be out there shaking hands every. . . "

A bell over the front door jingles as Nan enters. The sunlight streaming through the plate glass behind her ignites the alabaster sheen of her dress, creating a halo around her.

Harding smiles at his young visitor. "Well, hello there, miss."

"Good afternoon, Mr. Harding," she replies, shyly.

Old Abe rises, sniffs Nan's shoes. No one he knows. He waddles back to his rug.

"What can we do for you today?" asks Harding.

"I brought you a poem."

"A poem."

"Yes sir. For the *Marion Star's* 'Poem of the Week.'"

"And you wrote it? All by yourself?"

"Oh yes sir."

"Well if it's good, we just might publish it." Harding winks at Foraker. "Like to read it to us?"

Solemnly, Nan nods, slides a piece of paper from her pocket, and unfolds it. "It's called 'My True Love.'"

Harding smiles at her encouragingly. " 'My True Love.' Well, well. Let's hear it."

Nan begins reading to him in a small, clear voice. "My

True Love, by Nan Britton." She takes a deep breath, then plunges in.

"Upon a white steed there rides into my life
A man Fate had destined to make me his wife.
A blink of an eye and I'm under his spell.
From that moment on, in my soul he doth dwell."

"My, my," says Foraker. "'In my soul he doth dwell.' Please, go on child."

Nan draws another breath, then lets fly:

"Our lips meet in passion, our bodies entwine.
My mind is aswim in desire divine.
The heat of my heart exceeds that of the sun.
Two loins meld together as we become one."

Harding and Foraker exchange a look of astonishment. Nan ventures her first smile. "That's my poem."

A dense silence.

Harding clears his throat. "Yes. . . well. That's quite a—poem, er, Nan. Quite a poem. Yes indeedy."

Foraker nods.

Nan's green eyes glow. "Is it good enough, do you think? Good enough to be in the paper?"

Harding weighs his words. "Well, yes it's quite good." He pauses. "Not our usual thing, though. Most of our poems are more—actually, they're less. . . "

Nan's face falls.

Harding shifts gears. "But, er, sure. I think with—a little editing we could put it in. Is that all right? If we change it just a bit."

"Oh yes sir," replies Nan, brightening again. "Whatever you think best. Thank you."

Proudly she hands it over to him. Harding takes it, affectionately pats Nan's shoulder, and looks the poem over in continuing disbelief.

Foraker squints at the budding poetess. "How old are you, young lady?"

"Fifteen, sir. Just this month."

"Fifteen, fifteen. Hmmm."

"Yes, sir. Well, I have to go. My mother asks that I come straight home after school."

Harding nods. "That's good, Nan. Always listen to your mother." Again he clears his throat. "Your mother—she hasn't by chance seen this. . . ?"

"Oh no. You're the only one." Meaningfully, she looks up at him, her eyes deep green pools. "I wanted *you* to be my first." She gives him a smile that would set a glacier to the boil. "Well—good-bye, Mr. Harding." The merest glance at Foraker. "Good-bye, sir."

The front doorbell jingles as Nan returns to the street.

Foraker shakes his head. "You see? Teach young ladies to read and write— this is what you get."

3.

There are seven enjoying supper that evening at the Harding home, a three-story Queen Anne on Oak Street, though in fact contrarily set amongst century-old elms. The dining room, like the rest of the house, is redolent of Edwardian overstuffed, Midwestern comfort. Candles supplement the elemental electric lighting, neither yet any match for the setting sun, glowing through the leaded glass windows.

The host carves one last slice off a gigantic ham, then starts the platter of meat around the table. "Now all of you forget that bird for a moment," commands Harding. "Start on Doc's ham. You never in your life had ham like this."

He presides at one end of a well-supplied dining room table, his wife Florence, Harding's "Duchess," a full half-dozen years his senior, heavyset and sternly maternal, holding down the other. Joining them this warm summer night are Everett Sawyer, a crusty, spry general practitioner in his sixties; the Cartwrights, middle-aged long-time friends from across town; and a monied couple in their thirties, the Phillipses, Harding's next-door neighbors. And Old Abe lying in his usual place at his master's feet.

Jack Phillips eats little but drinks much, and has already settled into a stupor; he is hardly one to discern that his unexpectedly svelte and urbane wife, Carrie, sitting on Harding's immediate right, has difficulty keeping her eyes off the host. Florence Harding chooses not to notice. For the most part. "Doc Sawyer cured the ham himself," she boasts, on her guest's behalf.

"Have you a cure now for everything, Doctor?" asks Carrie, in a silken voice.

"Seem to do best with ham," Doctor Sawyer replies.

As the ham is passed along, Florence follows with a plate of creamed potatoes, ladling them out with a silver serving spoon, starting with the doctor. "Hardly anybody knows that you're just about the finest physician in Ohio, Doc, and they never will, less you quit being so modest. How long have you kept my one poor kidney agoin'?"

Harding's brows knit. Twenty years of marriage have yet to accustom him to his wife's directness. "My dear . . . !"

"Well it's true, Wurr'n. Weren't for Doc I'd a been laid out years ago."

Sawyer chuckles. "Florence, you and your one poor kidney will outlast us all."

"Not if she keeps pushing herself like she does," says Harding. "Top of everything else, she's taken to coming down to the paper again."

Florence argues her case to the entire table. "*Some*one has to oversee the accounts. Klein's hadn't sent a penny for its advertisements of *last Christmas*!" She and her creamed potatoes reach Carrie, who declines with the raising of a delicate hand—and nonetheless receives a triple portion, served with some force.

"Klein's been having its financial problems," Harding observes.

"Though in fairness," says Florence, resuming her seat, "it's been last Christmas since my husband's sent them a bill."

"We know they haven't the money," Harding persists, gently. "Why rub it in."

Florence shakes her head and holds out her palms in exasperation. Carrie looks ever more lovingly at Harding. He hastens to change the subject. "Meanwhile, it's election time again, isn't it? *Plenty* of notices there." He smiles reassuringly at Florence. "*All* paid in advance."

Just outside the Harding home, Nan comes pedaling her bike down the sidewalk, the last rays of sunlight winking off the spokes of the wheels, turning them to streaks of bronze. She stops at the front gate and gazes across the small lawn to the dining room window.

At least twice a day I would ride my bike past the Harding home on Oak Street and imagine his moving about in this room or that. I wondered what it might be like to be the lady of the house—preparing Mr. Harding's supper, ironing his clothes, chatting with him every day, taking in his words of wisdom. And touching him. Whenever I liked.

Inside, Carrie Phillips toys with similar thoughts as her slender fingers fondle a cigarette, much to Florence's unspoken disapproval. Few women in Marion have had a kind word for Carrie for the same reason men found her compelling—she possessed a succulent face that looked as if it had just come awake on an adjacent pillow. "Ever consider State office yourself, Warren?" Carrie asks.

"Absolutely not. . . "

"Certainly he has," insists Florence, simultaneously.

Harding shakes his head. "That's fine for folks who like stirring things up. I happen to think the world is getting along all right. Just as is."

Florence looks steadily at her husband. "Now Wurr'n, as I recall, only last week we talked about your running for governor."

"As I recall, one of us did all the talking."

Sawyer takes up the cause. "Well why the hell not, Warren? You've got so many boosters here and about. . . "

"Marion keeps re-electing you alderman year after year," adds Zach Cartwright.

Harding smiles modestly. "The more a politician actually does, good people, the more enemies he makes. Fortunately, an alderman doesn't really *do* anything. So, I get to keep my friends."

"My husband's driving ambition," says Florence with a sigh: "To travel from cradle to grave and never once give offense."

"Not so, Duchess, not so." Harding rises, plate in hand. "By God, I mean to have a second outsized helping of Doc's ham—and I'll knock over anybody who dares get in my way."

The sun has set hours ago but Nan is still at her post when the Hardings' front door opens. She rolls her bike behind a row of lilac bushes and peers through the leaves as the dinner guests make their farewells.

Sawyer and the Cartwrights start down the walkway. Carrie Phillips' hand lingers lightly in Harding's. Then the two Phillipses, he leaning drunkenly on her arm, cut across the small lawn to their house just next door, a massive stone structure with a slate roof. Old money.

At 10:00 P.M Florence is still persisting in her mission as she and Harding prepare for bed, he wriggling into a nightshirt, she in a nightgown, combing out her long gray hair. Florence homes in on the image of her husband, captive in her dressing table mirror. "If you just showed them a little interest. . . "

"My love. . . "

"You know they'd put you up for governor. . . "

"Duchess, I've just about everything a sensible man could want. Right here. What godly purpose would there be in moving to Columbus and starting over? Assuming I could get elected— which I can't."

She turns to face him directly. "You could, Wurr'n. Heavens sakes."

He shakes his head. "Truth is, most everyone in public life nowadays has been to college. Many have sat for the law. . . "

"You're smarter with words than all them over-educated fellas rolled together. Whenever anyone needs a speaker, who is it that they run to? And has anybody *once* asked where you've gone to school?"

"They can have *me* for free. Worth every penny, I might add. . . "

"People here hang on your every word. They look up to you. . . "

"All right, my dear. But this is just one small town. Ohio's a mighty big place." He folds down the bed covers. An ungainly medical apparatus of rubber and glass tubing—some sort of filtration system—stands at the foot of the bed. "When a man goes in to buy a suit, he gets a much closer fit if he knows his proper size. And the places where he might be a little—irregular." Tenderly, he kisses his wife's forehead. "Good night, Duchess. Hope you rest better."

And then Harding leaves their bedroom for the hallway and starts up the stairs to his own sleeping quarters, where he can be free of Florence's tosses and turns—and ambitions. He has not, in fact, slept with his wife for some years, and—the least introspective of men—no longer gives the matter much thought. Florence has yet to broach the subject and so, let sleeping dogs lie.

Alone in the master bedroom, Florence stares unhappily at her image in the dressing table mirror. Fingertips on her cheekbones, she lifts her cheeks and temples up and back, smoothing out her face. For a few moments she sees something of her younger, less forbidding self.

Twenty years ago, several things had inspired Florence to maneuver a young, malleable Warren Harding into marrying her, despite their substantial age difference. First, his arresting physical appearance, which to her eyes acquired an almost Olympian aura whenever he stepped out to address a crowd, suggested far more potential than that discernible in any other available man in Marion, irrespective of age; and she believed that her six-year advantage could only be an asset in her efforts to mold Harding's talents and secure his footing firmly on a steeply upward path—before he got too set in his ways. Beyond that, since childhood, Florence had never been able to abide anyone telling her "no," and Warren Harding was known for a willingness to travel across town by way of Cincinnati if he could thereby avoid turning someone down. In short, a perfect match.

During their courtship, Florence had a significant edge over the beehive of far younger women who were sweet on her beau, but who had all been brought up to sit demurely until suitors proposed to them: a woman could wait her entire life for Harding to act so momentously; Florence lacked the patience to wait for anything. Having thus gotten exactly what she sought, Florence now felt she was in no position to complain, two decades later, that in fact she seemed to end up with so little.

Outside, Nan maintains her vigil, glancing up as the light in a small third-floor bedroom goes on. Harding appears at the window. He raises it, gazes across to the Phillips' house, then draws the shade.

Nan's night watch has ended. She pushes off and pedals down the street.

As she disappears into the darkness, the front door opens and Harding slips out, a robe over his nightshirt. He pads down the porch steps and hurries across the lawn to the Phillips' house.

Their kitchen light blinks on. Harding smiles as he sees Carrie Phillips glide past her kitchen window over to a screen door. She swings it open. Wordlessly, Harding steps inside. They fall into each other's arms. The light goes out.

4.

The following Sunday, beneath a torrid noonday sun, Harding stands bareheaded on the old wooden dais of the Marion Fairgrounds, opening a rally for the re-election of U.S. Senator William B. Foraker with one of his laudatory stemwinders. The seasoned candidate himself holds center stage from a folding chair just behind his fulsom champion, flanked on one side by Leland Sinclair, Chairman of Sinclair Oil, and by Mrs. Foraker on the other, all of them attired in heat-defying elegance. Three perspiring, hugely well-fed Republican bigwigs bring the complement to an even half dozen, greatly testing the tensile strength of the pine flooring beneath.

It's a fine turnout, close to six hundred people. Florence, under her parasol, the Cartwrights, Carrie, and off in a far corner, Nan, all listen attentively from separate places in the moist, enthusiastic assembly.

I was fortunate to have been present when Mr. Harding took that first, small, unexpected step in his ascent to world acclaim. Perhaps I flatter myself but I think it safe to say that I recognized the portentiousness of the occasion well before that dear, modest man did himself. There were no recording devices in those days, of course, so his exact words have been lost to posterity; but I can still hear many of them ringing in my ears today, as if just spoken.

Harding's powerful unctuous voice is its own microphone. He is a fluent, if grandiose orator, never using two adjectives where four might do. Waves of verbiage wash through the crowd, inundating boaters, bonnets and parasols, soaking the patriotic bunting, the signs, posters and flags, till finally swamping the brass band awaiting its cue at the other end of the field. Harding concludes with the requisite flourish:

"And so, dear friends, I can aspire to no greater privilege than to be able to reintroduce this stalwart paragon, already so well known, universally respected, admired, yea loved in this great state that he has served so long and with such extraordinary distinction; an intrepid steward, who eats, drinks and breathes Ohio; a gallant champion of Ohio's interests, a tireless and incisive leader deeply committed to the needs of its people; a peerless and nationally esteemed statesman—who brings home the bacon. Ladies and gentlemen, your senator, my senator, a senator's senator: *U.S. Senator, William B. Foraker*."

Few of Harding's listeners are there for a close examination of the issues. His final hyperbole is met with unreserved cheers, applause, and shouts of "Foraker, Foraker." The band springs to life with a short burst of a Sousa march.

As Harding takes his seat, mopping his brow with a red handkerchief, the candidate rises, steps forward and nods at the crowd. All smiles, he basks for several moments in the acclaim, then holds up his hands. The music dies away.

Foraker is relaxed. Confident. After eighteen years in the Senate, one thing he knows is how to make a good speech. It has always been the same speech. Until today.

"Thank you, friends. Thank you." The crowd quiets down. Another "Thank you." Then Foraker readies his little surprise. "A politician has to exercise care when choosing the man to introduce him. Certainly don't want someone putting folks to sleep."

Laughter in the crowd. One citizen waves his straw boater. "Starting to feel kinda drowsy now, Bill." More laughs and scattered shouts of "We want Harding."

"On the other hand, have Alderman Harding make the introductions and you risk of finding yourself something of an anticlimax." Florence gazes up at the dais, her usually pale face flushed with excitement. Harding can only look sheepishly at his shoes. "Well," continues Foraker, "I predict you'll soon be hearing our alderman friend speak for himself." He pauses. "When we all persuade Warren Harding—to make the run for governor. And today we will, won't we!"

Harding nearly falls off his chair. Florence's head bobs up and down decisively as Foraker is swept away by his own rhetoric. "Two Republicans in the U.S. Senate, and a new Republican office-holder, Warren G. Harding, in Columbus. Now wouldn't that be God's divine plan here on earth?" The crowd applauds, whistles and begins chanting "Harding, Harding." Harding smiles uncomfortably and shakes his head slowly from side to side. Helplessly, he looks out over his admirers and at two of the three women who love him—Carrie, joining in the cheers, and Florence, her eyes closed, nodding as she bathes in the sweet sound of her husband's name.

Off almost by herself is the third, standing at the edge of this sea of galvanized Harding supporters, her pulse quick with exhilaration.

Isn't it strange how the least able are often the most ambitious, always tooting their own horns, while a truly exceptional man like my dear Mr. Harding could never perceive his own greatness.

It is almost 3:00 P.M when, with all the speeches finally concluded, Harding steps down from the dais and slowly makes his way through the well-wishers and back slappers towards his wife.

But like it or not, that summer Mr. Harding was to find himself in the race for governor. Not even he could resist the will of The People.

Florence reaches out to him, eyes afire, her jaw set.

5.

Charlie Forbes, Harding's closest chum since high school, could sell you just about anything if he himself believed in it. Since there is little Charlie wasn't prepared to believe, he made an outstanding living on the road, hawking everything from silk to sandpaper. But every two years for the past eight, he would cheerfully stay close to Marion for as many days as it took to handle details of his friend's pro forma bids for alderman. And now that Harding had gotten caught up in serious politics, Charlie is the uncertain candidate's first and only choice for campaign manager.

He does not disappoint. In short of a week, the energetic salesman has the heretofore drab, somnolent offices of the *Marion Star* dressed up in American flags—obtained well below cost—and plastered with posters demanding "Harding for Governor." A few more days and the *Star* is alive with nubile volunteers, Nan the most industrious of the group, all furiously stenciling signs and stuffing envelopes, hell-bent on marketing their distinctly hometown product to the entire state.

Charlie's severe myopia has never compromised his sharp eye for attractive women of any age, and he is quickly captured by Nan's flawless young face. So it is she whom he chooses to accompany him and the new candidate one evening to the Odd Fellows Lodge in Columbus for a campaign speech. There, while Harding spins out his homilies, Charlie supervises Nan closely as she bustles about a table in back, filling cups with lemonade, and setting out cookies, brochures, lapel pins and buttons.

Nan attacks her duties with solemn single-mindedness. Grateful for Charlie's instruction, she is blind to the repeated sidelong glances he shoots her through his thick spectacles. Nor does she appear to weigh the probable meager return on her efforts: for every man, woman and child in the half-empty room Nan has nailed up no fewer than two "Harding for Governor" posters, and has filled at least three cups. This indefatigable dedication, as much as her burgeoning beauty, quickly earns her a permanent place in Harding's small traveling entourage. Increasingly, she takes over for Florence, for whom sitting on a train or in an automobile over any distance has become ever more difficult.

I was thrilled to be asked to help in Mr. Harding's campaign all across the state. I got to go everywhere, my first real experience with life outside little Marion. I watched dear Mr. Harding shake hands with several thousand people from every walk of life. How taken they all were by him! His victory seemed assured.

But then, what happened was, well, the campaign ran out of money. Can you imagine? It seems a lot of the big contributors, corporations like Sinclair Oil and such, just weren't all that interested in Mr. Harding and what he stood for. Which is when I first learned that support of The People is of great importance, but in a large state like Ohio, money matters too. And we had nowhere near enough. Come the elections, sadly, incredibly, my darling lost.

The evening of his defeat, a dejected Harding is alone in his headquarters at the *Star* as he picks through the detritus of his failed campaign. All at once he has a sense of being observed, spins around, and finds Nan standing in the doorway.

"Why Nan—come in child. How're you doin' this evening?"

She enters. "In truth, I'm feeling rather badly, Mr. Harding."

"Now you shouldn't, my dear. I was always a long shot, you know. From start to finish. Probably had no business thrusting myself out there like that in the first place. But—everybody gave it their best, didn't we. That's all we can do."

"You would have been a wonderful governor, sir."

"I'm pleased you think so, Nan. Thank you." Wearily he climbs onto a chair and starts pulling down posters.

She goes for the broom in the corner and begins sweeping up. Harding acknowledges her efforts with a nod.

"That's real sweet of you. Florence was going to come by but she had to take to her bed this evening."

"You must be so tired, too. Please, let me get those posters. You have to keep yourself for the important things."

He chuckles. "Important things—what important things?"

Softly, Nan replies. "Your heart's desire."

"Really. My 'heart's desire.'" He turns back over his shoulder and looks at her closely. "I don't think I know what you mean, Nan."

"You simply listen to your heart. That's all you need to do. Your heart tells you what's most important in life and what's not. It doesn't care about momentary success or failure."

"Is that right?" Harding reflects for a moment. "And *your* heart's desire, child—what might that be, may I ask?"

Nan arrests her broom and looks him in the eye. "My heart's desire is that you be loved. Whatever else happened, wherever you went, I'd have you the most adored and happiest man on earth."

I don't know where on God's earth I found the cheek to say what I did to Mr. Harding, but there it was. And I was mighty lucky to have been given the chance that evening to speak my mind, for over the next two years I had to make do with seeing my darling from afar. He was, after all, a busy and important man, surely the most important man in Marion. And who was I? Scarcely more than a child. But my heart seemed undaunted by such considerations. He was always in my thoughts. Always, always.

And not infrequently in her sights.

One autumn evening, Nan straddles her bike under a canopy of red and gold leaves, spying from across the street as Harding slips out of Carrie Phillips' kitchen. She observes Harding stop and turn back just as Carrie comes to the door, his Panama in her hand. Carrie returns the hat to him with a furtive kiss, then watches with a loving smile as Harding once more starts towards his house. . . and at that moment, she spots Nan. The women's eyes connect. Abruptly, Nan pedals off.

A pair of snowmen sit out a February afternoon of light snow on a park bench directly across from the *Marion Star*. One has turnips for eyes and a carrot for a nose. Miraculously, the other has the power of locomotion—it's Nan, now sixteen, bundled up, thoroughly dusted with snow. Through the *Star's* storefront window she can see Harding playing poker with Forbes, Foraker, Sawyer and Cartwright. It's close to dinner time. Nan's mittened hand pulls out her companion's nose. She takes a loud bite. Her teeth crunching the carrot ring crisp and clear in the cold air.

The crack of a bat one bright morning the following spring finds Nan in the bleachers of Marion County's unprepossessing sports stadium, cheering for the home team as Harding's bat slams a baseball squarely. Harding, in Marion Maulers uniform, not only gets a home run off the hapless Columbus Cats, but drives in two others. Carrie Phillips, in the stands behind home plate, applauds as loudly as her white gloves will permit. Across the field, a kid in knickers and a cap changes the scoreboard:

Eighth inning, a total of seven runs for the home team, still zip for the Cats.

Nan, flanked by two would-be suitors, both smitten, both ignored, focuses intently on the game—or more accurately, on one particular player, though occasionally shooting a glance over at Carrie. One of Nan's admirers offers her a hot dog, the other some of his popcorn. Politely, she declines both.

It's a good twenty minutes before the Cats finally get their chance—their last chance—at bat. Harding, in catcher's gear, covers home plate.

The ball's in play. Columbus Cat Charlie Forbes, clearly no athlete, labors around third and struggles toward home. The throw from center reaches Harding in plenty of time for him to tag the plodding runner. But Harding appears to fumble the ball, and Charlie scores, triumphant, winded—and startled by his success. The kid revises the score board:

Bottom of the ninth, seven to one.

Up in the bleachers, Nan smiles at Harding's little act of charity, and falls yet more deeply in love.

I will confess, those teenage years of yearning were terribly difficult for me. I had all these feelings inside and no place to put them. I suffered horribly and in silence for, since Mr. Harding's campaign, we had not the opportunity to exchange a single word. Finally, I could contain myself no longer. Throwing propriety to the winds, I resolved to renew our acquaintance. Right then and there.

The game's lopsided conclusion is marked by a roar of approval and caps in the air as the players lope off the field. Mugs of beer make their way to both teams, admirers and hangers-on. Carrie's eyes twinkle as she watches Harding and several other players congratulate themselves expansively with handshakes and slaps on the back.

Harding spots a small boy in a sailor suit, baseball and stubby pencil in hand, shyly looking up at him, waiting for an autograph. He steps away from the men, signs the ball, and pats his young fan's head. As the youngster scoots back to his buddies, flaunting his trophy, Carrie strolls over. "Alderman Harding—don't think we didn't see you give that run away."

"Ah, Mrs. Phillips. I was certainly all thumbs there, wasn't I."

She moves closer, blinking up at him through her long eyelashes. "You're never all thumbs, Warren. In fact, I find your hands quite clever. . . "

"The end was in sight. We could afford to be generous."

Carrie purrs. "Might that renowned generosity of yours extend to me, do you think?"

"Now you know I can refuse you nothing."

"Perhaps this evening then?" she asks, conspiratorially. "What say later you and I slip over to. . . "

Abruptly, a breathless Nan pops up.

“Good afternoon, Mr. Harding. Remember me?” Nan’s chest heaves nervously, her adolescent’s blouse barely equal to her distinctly adult bosom.

Harding is delighted to see her, Carrie less so. “Well of course I remember you, Nan,” he says. “Hello. Thought that was you jumping up and down there in the bleachers. Mrs. Phillips, you’ve met little Nan Britton, haven’t you?”

“Oh yes. She’s not so little any more. Good to see you again Miss Britton.”

Nan and Harding engage, ostensibly reviewing the intricacies of the morning’s plays. Carrie, unwilling to join Nan and Harding’s conspiracy to deny the younger woman’s rampant sexuality, continues to smile and nod agreeably but all at once feels strangely removed from the conversation.

Understandably, my darling had many admirers. That lovely Mrs. Phillips, for example. How often I thought about how very wonderful it must be for her to have Warren Harding actually living right next door. But unexpected events were soon to take him from both of us, and from the neighborly town he loved so dearly.

6.

A short walk from the baseball diamond, a gaunt Senator Foraker sits alone and forlorn, drinking steadily at the bar of the Marion Clubhouse, hangout for Marion's movers and shakers. Men only.

Members come and go, some exchanging quick greetings with the solitary figure at the bar. Repeatedly, he tries waving them over. No takers.

A knickered golfer breezes in. Foraker calls out to him. "Hiram—good to see you. How's the twins?"

"Eating me out of house and home, Bill, house and home," says Hiram as he quickly passes on by. A second member hurries along right behind him, nodding at Foraker as he shoots past. "You're looking well, Senator," he lies, politely.

"I'm in the pink, Stu. Got time for a quick one?"

"Love to, Senator, but, uh, not today. Got this, uh, dental appointment."

Foraker returns morosely to his shot glass and empties it in a gulp. "Dental appointment," he mumbles as he motions to the bartender for a refill. Dusty heads of deer caught unawares and unarmed by sportsmen of decades past stare down at him with eyes as melancholy as his own.

Moments later, Harding and Charlie stroll in, spirits high, lugging their baseball equipment. Harding spots Foraker slouched over his glass. He sets down his bat and mitt, and joins his old friend at the bar. "Bill, where've you been keeping yourself?" Harding asks. "Missed a great game."

"Hullo." Foraker grasps Harding's hand as if it were a life preserver. "A friendly face at last. Been right here, right here. Quite some time now. Rest of the world's been hiding. Lemme treat you to one." Harding settles on an adjacent stool as the bartender approaches. "A double shot of Mr. Harding's favorite Kentucky mash, Mike," Foraker says, his speech slurred. "And I wouldn't mind a refill. Wouldn't mind at all."

"Coming up, Senator."

"Sure glad to see ya, Warren," says Foraker. "You'd think I had the friggin' plague."

"Believe me, Bill, this storm will pass. They all do. The People know you. You're like family. A man of your stature, the important. . . "

"'Fraid that counts about as much as a quart of monkey snot, Warren, my boy. Thing is, the higher up the pole you climb, the more people can see of your arse, know what I mean?"

"Now c'mon, Bill, you know there's a tremendous amount of respect. . . "

"Thought I had mine covered. Hell, I wrote those goddamn regulations." He hiccups. "Turns out those reformer bastards are going to strip me naked. Boil me in oil. Sinclair Oil." Another hiccup. "Forty-two years in elected office." His eyes fill with tears. "The only life I know. . . "

Mike approaches with Harding's drink, gives Foraker another. "Here y'are, Senator."

"Thanks, pal," says Foraker. He starts to lift his glass. Then slowly he puts it back down and places one hand over his forehead. "I don't feel very well, Warren."

"Yah—why don't we get you home. Mike—give us a hand here?"

Mike comes from around the bar and helps Harding get Foraker up and moving shakily toward the door. Foraker squeezes Harding's arm. "You've always known the meaning of loyalty, Warren. They don't make many like you. One in a million you are, one in a million. . . "

In the *Star's* front office the following day, Harding, news copy and blue pencil in hand, confers with his editor, Walt Harris, while on the other side of a frosted glass door, Florence despairs over the ledgers. Harding taps Walt's draft with his pencil. "Of course we have to report the facts." He frowns. "But the *wording*! '. . . William Foraker to stand trial on charges of malfeasance, accepting bribes. . . ' Good Lord!"

Tentatively, Walt defends integrity in journalism. "Those *are* the charges, boss."

Harding shakes his head. "How 'bout: 'It's alleged that certain of the Senator's acts were questionable, and entirely inconsistent with his usual high standards of legislative conduct.' And while you're at it, let's throw in something about the roads and bridges he's brought in for us last year, so on and so forth."

Walt gets on board. When first beginning work for the *Star*, he was troubled by Harding's blithe indifference to "the facts"; this was a newspaper, after all. But Walt quickly learned on which side the *Star's*—and his—bread was buttered. "We never hit a man when he's down."

"That's the spirit, Walt, that's the spirit." Harding hands him back the copy. "But more than that, Walt. If a man can't count on his friends. . . "

Walt nods and returns to the press room, just as the bell on the front door jingles, announcing the arrival of four men—Harry Daugherty and his adoring aide, Jess Smith, flanked by Leland Sinclair and Ralph McPherson, Ohio's Republican National Committeeman. McPherson, dripping, as always, with good cheer, sprints over to press Harding's hand between both of his own. "Alderman!"

"Ralph, Leland. . . gentlemen," exclaims Harding. "This *is* a surprise."

McPherson releases Harding's hand. "I believe you've met the distinguished barrister from Columbus, Harry Daugherty. . . "

"Uh—yes, wasn't it at Bill's last swearing-in. . . ?"

"His indispensable assistant, Jess Smith. . . "

"How d'ya do," squeaks Jess in a high, lisping tenor.

More handshakes.

Florence, hunched over her accounts, sits up straight as unfamiliar voices leak through the wall. Quietly, she rolls her chair closer to the door, cupping an ear, as the *Star's* prestigious visitors settle in. Harry Daugherty and Jess Smith arrange themselves together on the old loveseat, the only visible hint of their longstanding, clandestine coupling.

Harding remains on his feet, half leaning against, half sitting on the desk "So—what may I do for you folks, today?"

McPherson takes charge. He is more oppressively genial than usual. "Warren—don't know how you manage to put out a newspaper week after week, year after year, and never get anyone mad at you. But you do."

For Harding, the supreme compliment. "Why, thank you, Ralph. No point stepping on a man's toes when there's so many other spots to place your feet. . . "

"You mind your own business, sir," McPherson continues, "that's what it is. Rare in a journalist these days."

"Well, just seems to me, with so much good news to report, I hardly have time to go around trying to scare up . . . "

Leland Sinclair stirs. "And the *Star's* fidelity to the senator during his current—difficulty is particularly appreciated. I speak for my entire board."

"Bill Foraker is a fine man," says Harding. "No doubt about that."

"Yes," says McPherson. "A fine man."

McPherson appears to have run down. A long moment of silence. The air hangs heavy.

Daugherty, his large, spherical, nearly hairless head perched on his high-winged collar like a casaba melon, has been sitting quietly, studying Harding with heavy-lidded eyes that miss little. Ever so lightly, he drops the first shoe. "Regrettably, under the circumstances, the senator has felt obliged to withdraw his candidacy."

McPherson drops the second. "Warren, we very much want you to run in his place." Harding flinches visibly, but McPherson presses on. "Even with your long friendship, you're personally untainted by the senator's—misfortunes . . . "

"Never get all them reformer types riled. . . " adds Jess Smith, his voice an octave above the rest.

"In fact," continues McPherson, "I can't think of a single credible reason anyone might have to vote against you, can you?"

Harding shakes his head. "Seems folks found all kinds of reasons just two years ago, when I made that fool bid for governor. Talk about overreaching. Fellas, please don't think me unappreciative. I'm flattered, I truly am, but I'm afraid the answer. . . "

Daugherty doesn't wait for the answer. "Point is, it won't be easy for *any* Republican this year. But, *properly* financed," he glances meaningfully at Sinclair, "you may well be our best chance to keep Bill's seat. You got a duty to your party, sir."

McPherson nods vigorously. "And to our good mutual friend. Bill specifically asks that it be *you* who carries on his great work. Says you're one man we can always count on. He's sure right about that."

Daugherty delivers the coup de grace. "It all comes down. . . it all comes down to a question of *loyalty*."

McPherson gives Harding his most ingratiating smile. "Well, *Senator* Harding, what d'ya say?"

Seconds tick by. Harding seems unable to say anything.

And then the inner office door flies open and Florence bursts in. "He says *yes*, gentlemen, of course, Senator Harding says *yes*."

That night, sultry and still, finds Nan holding down her park bench opposite the *Star*. Never before has she had to stand watch this late. Since her arrival a good two hours ago, a full moon has risen, lending her a distinct shadow. Harding's dark offices appear empty.

Sitting alone in the lightless back room amongst his silent presses, Harding stares unseeing at the typesetter. What many men would consider uncommon opportunity has somehow brought him a sense of profound loss, even foreboding—another chance to fail. Yet, how could he be so ungracious as to turn the boys down? What would they all think of him? And poor Duchess—she'd probably take to her bed again for weeks.

Finally Harding rises, passes through the front office, takes his Panama from the rack and trudges out of the building, Old Abe at his heels.

Old Abe was not only Harding's third consecutive Airedale but the third to be named Old Abe. Not ordinarily a man of passion, all his life Harding fervently despised change. A thaw in February and a cold snap in July were equally unsettling. He fretted if Florence failed to find a decent chicken for their Sunday dinner; Sundays and chicken seemed to him inseparable. He resisted buying new trousers till its predecessor had been worn thin to the point of transparency. He despaired if a favored pair of shoes were finally beyond repair. He had yet to see where a phone-call might serve better than a letter, and though he now conceded the utility of Duchess having their home electrified, the wiring had been entirely her initiative, done over his protests, all with her own money.

But these were transient vexations, easily managed. On balance, Harding had designed a safe, satisfying life of iron-clad predictability and calm. His Tuesday and Friday night unions with Carrie Phillips were adventure enough for any man. In all things, Harding never felt the need to push himself or test the limits, attempting only what was sure to go well. Thoroughly comfortable with his place in the sun, not yet fifty, he had achieved his apotheosis, extracting from life precisely what he wanted: peace and quiet.

That is, until today. Whatever in God's name had he let himself in for this time? Hadn't he done his bit for the party with that foolish run for governor? His father had always warned him—go out on a limb and someone's sure to come along with a saw. Now here he was, sticking way out there. *Way* out. Warren Harding, sacrificial lamb. Warren Harding—public idiot!

Nan watches Harding leave the *Star* and head down the street. She stands and falls in behind him.

He comes to a street-corner, where a ragamuffin approaches, palm out. Harding digs into his pocket and gives the boy a handful of coins. They glitter in the moonlight. Then he resumes his steps, turns left, stops, changes his mind and turns right, toward the fairgrounds.

The cicadas are shouting at one another as Harding wanders onto the baseball diamond. Nan continues to observe unseen as he picks the broken limb of a tree off the ground and shuffles over to home plate, the site of many a weekend triumph. He raises the limb to his shoulder and takes an imaginary pitch.

There was no way I could then know of the worries weighing down so mightily upon Mr. Harding that last year he was to live in Marion, though I could see that he faced a problem of some magnitude, and that it was bringing him great distress. How I wished I could have run to him with a word of comfort, or perhaps just held his hand that soft summer night. But I was a mere sixteen. I could do nothing, save entrust this dear man to the many others in his life who I believed surely loved him as did I, and would do all they could to ease his cares.

Harding sighs deeply, lowers the branch, and breaks it over his knee.

7.

Unfailingly on time for her twice monthly 11:00 A.M. glimpse into the future, Florence Harding, in hat and veil, stands on the front steps of a small corner two-story wood frame house. She glances to her left, then to her right. Satisfied she's gone unnoticed, she spins the bell. A forty-ish woman, matronly in appearance and dress, opens the door and with a nod, bids Florence enter. Nothing about her or her unassuming home would suggest that it is here, at the confluence of Marion's Third and Main, that the fate of the world was consistently and reliably revealed.

The woman shows Florence through a parlor and on into the kitchen where they seat themselves at opposite ends of a small maplewood table covered with a gingham cloth. An octagonal wall clock ticks domestically. Without fanfare, the woman spreads out a pack of cards. Everything is low-key, matter of fact. No hocus pocus. This, after all, is Ohio.

Today, Florence has a very specific question for her. "Madam, you must tell me. . . "

The woman, as we might expect, is well ahead of her. "Ah yes, it is *quite* clear, Mrs. Harding," she says, her voice full of promise.

"It is?"

"Your husband continues to draw upon many powerful forces. They propel him forward at great speed. His progress now seems inevitable."

Florence looks at her triumphantly. "So then, he—he *will* succeed. That's what you see, isn't it," she insists. "I've always known it. In my heart."

The woman nods in agreement, though smiling cryptically. She slowly picks up a card and examines it in silence, then another, and another. Still, she says nothing. The wall clock marks off the seconds.

Florence cannot contain her impatience. "Yes? Well, what do they say?"

But the woman takes her time. With clairvoyance

comes responsibility—one doesn't go off half cocked. When at last she speaks, her words are measured. "This magnetism of your husband's—it gathers up people's dreams. Helps them to come true." She pauses and then adds, cautiously, "but perhaps not always *his* dreams."

"Wurr'n has no dreams," asserts Florence. "I mean, he's never been a dreamer. He, he only wants—what any capable man would. Just that, at times he's lacked confidence. In his abilities. But I've always had faith."

The woman rearranges the cards, gleaning yet another insight. "Your faith is well placed," she says, softly. "So long as you remember, Mrs. Harding: there is balance in the universe; for every great force there is a countervailing power." She looks up at her again. "Nothing is ever without cost. There is always a reckoning."

8.

Even the most celebrated of journeys can begin with steps so small as to be imperceptible. How many of us at an unheralded gathering that day in an inconsequential Ohio town might have predicted where Mr. Harding's road would ultimately lead? And despite my fantasies, how could I possibly have divined that we would be traveling that ascendant road together?

Nan, ever more reluctantly in the company of her father, is in the genial crowd of nearly two hundred clumped around Marion's courthouse steps, waiting deferentially for the "Harding for U.S. Senate" kickoff rally to begin. Mr. Britton excepted, Harding's popularity seems to touch young and old, and cuts across every strata of Marion society. For the most part, the attendees are day-workers, small businessmen, farmers and the like, but here and there are the decidedly well-to-do, several sitting in horse-drawn carriages or in chauffeured motorcars. Behind the wheel of her electric, Carrie Phillips is among the last arrivals, silently rolling up to take her place with the monied set. Peering down at them all from the makeshift dais at the top of the old granite stairs are Harry Daugherty, Jess Smith, Ralph McPherson, and Charlie Forbes—but thus far, no Harding.

Right on schedule, a brass marching band approaches, blasting away at John Philip Sousa. Daugherty glances at a pocket watch, then turns to Charlie. "Where the hell's our candidate?" Charlie stabs his forefinger in the direction of the band's tuba player. Daugherty shakes his head as he discovers that Harding is performing at his own rally.

The crowd cheers as the tuba bobs into view. Several moments later, the musicians reach the courthouse and halt on command. Harding passes his battered instrument to a band mate and sprints up the steps to applause and shouts of approval, then shakes hands with all on the podium as Charlie moves forward to introduce him.

Harding lays a restraining hand on his friend's shoulder.

"Hey thanks, pal, but just about everyone knows me pretty well, don't you think? For better or worse." He clears his throat, turns, faces his audience and warms it with his smile. He's known most of these people all his life. This would be the easy part. "Afternoon good people. I sure do appreciate you sparing the time to come over today."

Supportive murmurs rise up to him. Harding can make out "Hullo, Warren," and "Glad to be here." Carrie Phillips gives him a discreet wave.

"Guess you've all heard, some gracious folks contend that I might make Ohio a pretty fair United States Senator."

A heckler's voice rings out. "*They must know something we don't!*" Good-natured laughter from the crowd, a lethal look from Nan. The heckler is her father.

"That may be, Mr. Britton, that may be," responds Harding, amiably.

"*Don't take any guff, Warren,*" shouts Marion's greengrocer. "*You're gonna make one hell of a first-class senator!*"

"Thank you, Rufus. And I'm sure anxious to get cracking, folks—get down to doing. . . doing what we all know needs to be done in Washington. For every one of you good people. But I make you this promise: If elected, one thing will never change: my home is here. In Marion. So I'll be coming back. A lot. We'll chat. Like we always have. I'll want to hear about *your* problems. What I can do to help. Tell me whenever I'm off the beam."

"*You can count on it, Harding*!" hollers Nan's father.

"And first thing, Mr. Britton, I'm gonna create a special complaint bureau here in town. Just for you."

Over the ensuing laughter, Jess Smith murmurs in Daugherty's ear. "Guy knows how to work a crowd."

"This little crowd, yeah," replies Daugherty. "Trouble is, he still thinks he's running for alderman."

The rally over and a considered success, the atmosphere in Harry Daugherty's chauffeured La Salle is celebratory as he and Harding, McPherson, and Jess Smith motor down Main Street. Charlie Forbes, asked at the last minute by McPherson to run him a "small errand," is notably absent, freeing McPherson to make his move. "Warren, I'm sure I don't have to tout Harry here—his legendary accomplishments—the wealth of political knowledge and experience . . . "

"Ran Senator Foraker's last two campaigns," interposes Jess, reverently.

"Knowledge and experience he's happy to make available to you," finishes McPherson.

Harding turns to Daugherty. "Well gosh, Harry, that's quite generous. Lord knows I could certainly use your help. Yes indeedy." He pauses. "Thing is. . . "

"Yes?" asks Daugherty, the slightest edge to his voice.

"Well, about Charlie," Harding replies. "Charlie's taken charge of all my previous campaigns. Been elected alderman four times, ya know. . . "

"We know, Warren, but we're talking national office now," says McPherson.

Daugherty is a model of conciliation. "You keep Charlie on. That's fine. We'd be doing very different things. I'll be coaching the in-field. We'll have Charlie keep an eye on the out-field."

"Just wouldn't want to hurt his feelings, that's all," says Harding. "Charlie and I go way back. . . "

"Hurt his feelings? No, we certainly wouldn't want to hurt his feelings." Daugherty pauses. "So long as you and I have an understanding. Can't have six different people making decisions, can we."

Daugherty's chauffeur, Bobby Burns, a muscular, pugnacious man—a pitbull in shoes—eavesdrops as the men seated behind him shove Harding's lifelong friend to the periphery of the campaign. A licensed private detective permanently on Daugherty's payroll, he has come to admire his employer's genteel use of force. In his youth, Burns had been partial to other forms, though even then always applied judiciously—why kill a man when your point might easily be made by breaking his knees? Now in his maturity, he has developed a keen interest in Daugherty's subtler tactics, if not totally abandoning his own more physical instincts.

Fifty yards ahead, an elderly woman steps off the curb, inattentive to the slowly approaching La Salle. The boulevard is wide, the traffic negligible—room for Burns to miss her by a dozen yards. Instead he turns the wheel slightly, bearing down upon her. The right front fender brushes the woman's skirt as the huge motor car glides by. Burns smiles, gratified by his precision driving and his victim's fright.

Behind him, Daugherty, focused on his mission, remains unaware of his chauffeur's pastime. Having despatched Charlie, he can concentrate all his fire power upon the candidate himself. "There's a few other details I thought we might get straight, Warren. If that's all right." He nods at Jess Smith, who pulls out a pad and begins taking down notes.

"Sure," says Harding. "Let's have 'em."

"First off, your little friendship with—I'm told her name is Carrie Phillips. . . ?" Harding's jaw drops. Smoothly, Daugherty continues. "You'll want to keep it under wraps, okay? Till the campaign's over. Second, we need more photographs. You're a great speechifier but one good picture can obscure a thousand words. Pictures of you with children. Photogenic young people. I understand you and the missus are childless?"

"Well, uh, yes. Florence's health has never. . . "

"We'll find you some."

"Er, find me some?"

"Some children. Youth—innocence sells. Appearances—that's what politics are about now, Warren. Photographs. And we'll need one of 'The candidate walking his dog.' Voters all love dogs."

"I have a swell dog. . . "

"Let me pick the dog," says Daugherty. He pauses. "One last thing."

"All right. Let's have it."

"These—whispers I've heard from time to time."

Harding's anxiety rises precipitously. "Whispers?"

"That you might be part colored."

Even McPherson is aghast at Daugherty's blunt incivility and looks away. Up front, Burns' ears strain for every detail.

"Harry," says Harding, "that cockeyed rumor has dogged my family for generations. We have no idea what started it."

"Sure. Is it true?"

"Of course not!" Harding turns and stares unseeing out the window. "I don't know. Maybe a hundred years ago one of my people jumped the fence. Who the hell's to say? Christ, I am who I am. Anyway, no one's ever taken that stuff seriously."

A strained silence, finally broken by Jess. "He sure don't look Negro. I gotta say, Mr. Harding, you look exactly like I always imagined a United States senator should."

Daugherty studies Harding's profile for a moment. "You're certainly right about that, Jess."

McPherson joins in. "And as you say, Harry, appearances count. For everything."

9.

***Some**thing sure counted. This time my prayers were answered. Mr. Harding was elected by a landslide. No ifs, ands, or buts.*

All was not well with me, however. I must tell you, I quickly found that there was a part of my heart that could not share in the outpouring of joy that followed. For when the voters delivered my darling to the United States Senate, they sent him far, far away from me. So thrilled though I was, for days I just sat and cried. I couldn't seem to stem the tears. Who knew when I might see Mr. Harding again? But I tried to take solace in the knowledge that this fine and worthy man was where he properly belonged, and was sure to prosper in the company of like statesmen.

Harding's first morning on the job, Ohio's senior senator, an avuncular Morris Webb, guides his awed colleague through the corridors towards the Senate chamber, introducing him to members they encounter, each and every one white, male, Protestant, prosperous, and ranging in years from middle-aged to senescent. Several, in office for decades, Harding already recognizes. None are more striking than New Mexico's Albert Fall, towering in height, if not legislative acumen, today replete with a ten-gallon Stetson, boots, string tie, and a wad of tobacco in his cheek.

Fall slaps Harding on the back. "Been lookin' forward to your arrival, Warren. Have I heard correctly that you play a crafty game of five-card stud? The poker caucus could use some fresh blood."

Webb chuckles. "You mean some fresh cash, don't you Al?"

Harding shakes his head. "Poker is one pleasure I may have to forego while I'm here, Senator Fall. The missus has made it quite clear. Can't afford to leave the Senate any less well-off financially than I am already."

"Why don't ya call me Al," says Fall. "And let me

assure you, friend, that in the century and a half of this august body's proud existence, no member has *ever* left less well-off financially than when he arrived." He slaps Harding's back a second time, and continues on his way.

Harding and Webb move on, encountering Fall's very antithesis, sixty-six-year-old Henry Cabot Lodge, an austere Boston Brahmin, barely five feet, thin, pinched, exacting, effete in dress and manner, and certain in the knowledge that God—if not the electorate—has long been saving him for the presidency of the United States.

"Warren, doubtless you know our majority leader?"

An enormous privilege, Senator Lodge," says Harding, with a perceptible bow.

Lodge's handshake is stiff and formal, the tone of his speech one of suppressed rage. "Most pleased to have you in the club," Lodge replies in his clipped Bostonian. "This institution needs more strong Republican voices, what with Professor Woodrow Wilson and his internationalist clique infesting the White House. I'll be counting on your help in preparing some enlightening lessons for the good professor."

"Well," says Harding, "I, uh, certainly want to do all I can. . . "

Lodge resumes his steps. "Splendid. Tea in my chambers at five, gentlemen?"

He's gone without bothering for an answer.

Moments later, Webb and Harding reach the Senate floor. Webb is a tolerant, closet moderate in an increasingly reactionary Republican party, and one of the few with something approaching a sense of humor. He points to an ornate door off to one side. "The Senate Dining Room, Warren. Avoid at all costs. The food's prepared entirely by civil servants—doesn't so much sate as *kill* the appetite."

They continue down a side aisle toward their desks. Just across the aisle, a dandy sporting a startlingly huge pompadour settles behind his. "Marcus Blakewood, New Jersey," Webb whispers. "Working on marriage number five, I believe. A Senate record. Even for a Democrat."

"Five marriages. . . !"

"Marcus is a man of intense but brief enthusiasms." As they approach, Blakewood gives them a friendly wave. "And don't be taken in by all this cordiality," warns Webb, softly. "Makes it that much harder distinguishing friends from mortal enemies."

Harding looks at him. "Enemies? Here? That's the last thing in the world I intend to have."

"You're to be in Washington for quite some time, Warren." Webb smiles. "Never know— you just might develop a taste for them."

PART TWO

10.

Sad to say, during the first few years of Mr. Harding's term in the Senate, despite his fondest wishes, he found little time to visit Marion. I had only the poor comfort of seeing his dear face in the newspapers. Yet, my feelings for him continued to grow; intense yearnings, unspeakable desires I could not share with a living soul.

Then one day, on impulse, I took pen in hand. It was probably a rather silly letter, all Marion gossip and the like. But it provided a decorous reason for me to boldly inscribe in green ink **"Dear Mr. Harding,"***—and then picture my darling's eyes reading those words.*

Joy of joys, he actually wrote me back—several lovely lines on the letterhead of the United States Senate! After regaining my composure, I wrote him again. Soon I was up to a letter a day. Many I dared not mail, but the little chatty ones, I did. Now and again he answered, and I would read his sweet words over and over.

As for the rest of my time, I just made do with my memories and my dreams, while keeping busy in my auntie's millinery. Till finally I had two hundred dollars put aside—enough for a trip to Washington, D.C. My first ever. Of course, spending several years' savings on such a venture could hardly please my father, who habitually referred to the capital of our nation as "that den of iniquity." But since no one in living memory had ever heard a murmur of approval from his lips—about any place, anyone, or anything—his predictable condemnation of my intended excursion had the effect upon me of a raindrop falling in the Sahara.

Carrying two new suitcases, Nan makes her way along the platform of Marion's train station, crowded, bustling, and everywhere adorned with World War I exhortations—*"BUY LIBERTY BONDS," "ROUT THE KAISER,"* and *"UNCLE SAM WANTS YOU!"* At twenty-one, she has come into a stunning maturity, as thoroughly observed by a homeward-bound row of disabled doughboys.

And so, the moment had come to surprise dear Mr. Harding with a little visit—to see with my own eyes the splendid things my senator was doing for America.

Largely, what Nan's senator was doing was prudently keeping out of America's way. Predictably, the day of Nan's unannounced arrival, like so many days before, Harding is secure in his office, wreathed in cigar smoke, a glass of bourbon close by, immersed in a poker game with Albert Fall and a trio of other legislative lightweights, Senators Paxton, Guthrie and Blair. Fall tosses a couple of bills on the mound accumulating on the table. "I'll see you. Raise you five."

"Warren?" asks Paxton.

"I'm out."

"Too rich for my blood," says Guthrie.

Harding and Guthrie fold their cards. A buzzer sounds.

"Christ," says Fall, "not now. I thought Henry had his quorum."

Fall, Blair and Paxton continue on with the game.

"See you, Al," says Blair. He throws several bills on the table. "And raise you another five."

There's a knock on Harding's door. A senatatorial page opens it a crack and sticks his head in. "Pardon me, gentlemen. Gonna be a voice vote. Mr. Lodge needs two more."

Fall is unmoved. "I'm sure as hell not going to fold this hand for a lousy seaport tariff bill. New Mexico's land-locked."

Harding rises. "Maybe if I get out of here now I'll at least keep my shirt."

Guthrie joins him. "Already lost mine. Guess I'll tag along."

Presiding over the senate, Lodge has scraped together his quorum—some two dozen senators are in their places, prepared to do their leader's bidding. Harding and Guthrie reach their desks moments before the roll call reaches them.

"Senator Guthrie?" asks Lodge.

"Guthrie votes no."

"Senator Hall?" Lodge continues.

"Hall votes no."

"Senator Harding?"

"Harding votes no."

Harding's modest three-word speech elicits wild applause from a young woman in the gallery. Startled senators look up in unison. With fifty eyes upon her, Nan freezes mid-clap and shrinks into her seat. Harding smiles up at her. Their eyes connect.

But neither is able to find a way to acknowledge the voltage between them as, early that evening, they dine together in the Willard Hotel's Potomac Room. Seated opposite Harding in the most splendiferous restaurant she has ever seen, Nan struggles with a bill of fare the size of a Tolstoy novel. A tuxedoed waiter looks on paternally. Harding sips his second bourbon. Nan's sarsaparilla is untouched. She peeps out at him from behind her menu. "This is so kind of you, Mr. Harding. It all looks so good. My oh my."

Harding nods. "Everything *is* good. What is it you want, my dear?"

What I wanted was for him to reach out to me, to lift me up into his arms and hold me. Right there. In that restaurant.

"Gosh, sir, so many things. How do you possibly choose? Have you decided?"

"I always have the Delmonico. The best in Washington."

I hadn't the slightest idea if the Delmonico was fish or fowl, but little else on the menu was recognizable either.

"Well, if you think it's that good, I must have the same."

"Oui, Mademoiselle. And how shall your Delmonico be prepared?" asks the waiter.

"Prepared?" repeats Nan.

"Oui, Mademoiselle."

"Perhaps. . . medium," suggests Harding.

"Yes, medium," enthuses Nan. "A splendid idea."

Harding nods at the waiter who thanks them both and departs with their order.

Nan and Harding look at each other, then down at the table. She shifts uneasily in her seat.

It is, of course, a sin to feel as I did about another woman's husband. But it was never my intention to entice Mr. Harding away from his honor-bound conjugal duty; I wished only to add to his life those parts of my love he found worthy—to give to him in some way, not to take.

Harding fiddles with his swizzle stick. "Where did you say you were staying, Nan?"

"At the Shepherd's Residence for women. On D Street."

"Rather posh."

"I'll say. I've barely enough money for a week. But my train ticket home is all paid. . . "

"I see. A week. So short." He looks at her. "Do you. . . *have* to go back to Marion?"

"Well, I—I guess. I never imagined. . . "

"I was thinking, Nan," says Harding slowly. "Possibly you'd like to stay on a bit? In Washington. We could find you a less expensive room, then get you a job. . . "

"In—in Washington. . . !"

"Yes, I believe we could come up with something for you here. Perhaps at the Republican National Committee."

I thought I'd died and gone to heaven.

"Gosh, Mr. Harding, that would be wonderful. 'Cept that—well, the only paying job I've ever had has been my auntie's little hat shop. I—I really don't know how to *do* anything."

"This is Washington, my dear—you'll fit in quite nicely."

A terrific din—car horns, church bells and shouts from the street outside increasingly penetrate and begin to fill the restaurant. Diners chatter excitedly to each other as the waiter approaches, wheeling a silver cart bearing rolls and butter.

Harding looks up at him. "What in blazes is going on out there?"

"I'm told it's the war, Monsieur. Rumor is, the Bosch are fini."

"What?!" Harding jumps up, grabs Nan's arm, virtually lifts her from the chair and leads her out onto Pennsylvania Avenue and bedlam. Sidewalks and roadway are choked with people in ecstatic disbelief—cheering, dancing, and hugging strangers. Church bells clang drunkenly.

Harding collars an animated young man. "What have you heard?"

"They say the Heinies quit. Kaiser's fled Berlin, tail between his legs. He's a Dutchman now. And my brother's coming back from France! While he's still in one piece." He dashes off.

Harding shakes his head. "Four years of slaughter. Pointless slaughter. Over. It's hard to believe."

"I'm so glad," says Nan.

No, not glad. I was delirious! For I was standing quite close to Mr. Harding, closer than I ever had before. With the crowd pressing in all around us we were soon squeezed together, my breasts hard against my darling. I felt two hearts beating, two hearts beating as one. I was dizzy, drowning in his manly scent that was suffused with bay rum and the lingering fragrance of his last cigar. I could hardly breathe. The surrounding tumult appeared to fade away and I was entirely alone with him. I heard nothing, saw nothing, felt nothing. . . save him.

Harding joyfully kisses the top of Nan's head, backs his face away for a second, looks into her eyes—then wraps his arms around her. Nan's arms encircle Harding's neck. They kiss fiercely, their bodies immobilized as they meld together, while seemingly all Washington hollers and whirls around them.

11.

Till my dying day I shall remember our first kiss that glorious night we learned that the Great War had ended. It felt for a moment as though we might actually consummate our love. Right then and there. On Pennsylvania Avenue. Lord in heaven, I was burning up inside. But after that one passionate moment, my dearest's conduct was so courtly, so protective, I remained quite chaste. In fact, it began to look as if I might well retain my maidenhood forever.

Less than a week after her arrival, Harding conducts a delighted Nan, clutching a box of candy and a small cellophane-wrapped bouquet of roses, through a small, simply furnished flat, fresh flowers in every room. Harding points out the living room window view of the Jefferson Memorial, then leads the new tenant through to the bedroom. Conspicuously, Nan sits herself down on the bed. She bounces on the mattress. But her guide appears caught up in the virtues of her walk-in closet, then he waves them on towards the kitchen.

Even a comprehensive tour of a one-bedroom apartment is bound to be brief. In a few minutes, Harding stands with Nan at the front door, preparing to leave. She faces him, arms at her side, quivering slightly. Tenderly he kisses her forehead. She closes her eyes, opens them. . . he's gone.

True to his word, my darling not only located a lovely place to live, he found me a wonderful position with the Republican National Committee. Would you believe that the job of junior assistant clerk paid more in a week than I earned in my auntie's shop an entire month! Best of all, there was I, Nan Britton from little Marion, Ohio, now never far from Senator Warren G. Harding, and other of America's greatest minds as they grappled majestically with momentous issues.

Henry Cabot Lodge reserved every Tuesday afternoon at four to meet with such great minds as could be found in the Senate Republican Caucus, gathering his loyal minions around a massive rectangular cherrywood table whose polished surface shone brightly, less so the intellect of some who regularly sat alongside. On this particular Tuesday, the occasion of a short but singularly historic meeting, the senators have all been supplied with copies of Woodrow Wilson's Versailles Treaty, a formidable stack of some one hundred pages of very small print. Several read parts of the treaty to themselves with visible distaste. Senator Guthrie taps a page with his pen. "This 'League of Nations' Wilson proposes—it's a pipe dream."

Murmurs of agreement, most vociferously from Senator Paxton. "Or worse," he asserts. "Give it an army to enforce its decisions and it's a threat to our sovereignty. No army, and it's a debating society—useless, utterly useless."

All around the table, near unanimous growls of animosity. But Morris Webb gently dissents. "Better useless debate than useless war, don't you think? And without the United States, the League would be very useless indeed."

A strained silence.

Pained to see his Ohio colleague dangling all by himself, Harding hurries to his support. "Morris makes an interesting point there. What with most every country in the world on board, can we stay out?"

Fall shakes his head. "I take it, Warren, you'd have Borneo sending a delegation of goddamn cannibals to argue beef quotas with New Mexico. . . "

Lodge stirs slightly, all he need do to elicit the group's undivided attention. "I have a more fundamental concern, gentlemen: does the United States wish to be embroiled again in the pernicious affairs of other nations, perhaps get dragged into another European war? What happens across an ocean somewhere is none of our business. And ours is none of theirs."

General nods of agreement around the table.

Webb tries again. "Possibly—there's a compromise here—that we join the League *in principle*—but reserve our right to act independently whenever it best serves our sovereign interests."

Compromise—Harding's lode stone. "Yes, Henry, a

compromise. There's something appealing, don't you think, about a forum where countries can sit down man to man. . . "

Paxton interrupts impatiently. "Warren, with *this* president it's all or nothing. You know Wilson doesn't compromise."

"Nor will I," says Lodge. "Wilson thinks to ram his League of Nations down our throats. That *alone* would be reason for Republicans to oppose—and oppose unanimously."

"So moved," says Guthrie.

"Second?" asks Lodge.

"Second," says Paxton.

"All in favor?" asks Lodge.

Save for Harding and Webb, the entire group votes "aye." Moments later Ohio's tentative spark of internationalism is extinguished, as the two holdouts hasten to add their votes to the others.

"Against?"

Lodge ventures his first smile in public since the Treaty of Versailles crossed his desk two months ago. "Well then—the 'ayes' have it."

He lifts the face sheet off Woodrow Wilson's blueprint for a permanent and lasting peace, an imaginative, daring plan not just to fairly settle up accounts of this war, but to anticipate and root out probable causes of the next.

Lodge ceremoniously tears the sheet in half.

12.

Carrie Phillips notes with vicarious satisfaction that the building housing the *Marion Daily Star* has been freshly painted, and the gold letters etched on the front window reflect further the paper's newfound prosperity:

MARION DAILY STAR
Warren G. Harding, Publisher
Walter Harris, Editor-in-Chief
Circulation 140,000

But when, through the plate glass, she spots a familiar Panama hat on the rack, her pulse quickens.

Inside the composing room, Harding, sleeves rolled up, happily sets a page of lead type with skill undiminished by a four-year absence. Walt Harris looks on, amused. The front doorbell jingles, and Harding recognizes a honeyed voice he's not heard for some time.

"Warren —?"

"In here." Carrie enters and Harding jumps up, clasping both her hands in his with great warmth. "Carrie, my dear . . . "

"Senator Harding, as I live and breathe. Good morning, Mr. Harris."

"Morning, Mrs. Phillips." Walt grapples conspicuously with his pocket watch. "Chief, I've got to, uh, get down to the grange." He turns mock serious. "Now—no dilly dallying. I'll need that finished by three o'clock. At the *latest*."

"Yes *sir*" says Harding. "I'll see what I can do."

Walt withdraws.

"What a lovely surprise, Warren," says Carrie. "We thought you weren't due in Marion until tomorrow."

"Yes, well I managed to slip out a little ahead of recess. Those final days—why don't you have a seat there—such a flurry of pork. Every senator wanting his. It's a disgrace. So this time I thought I'd just leave a bit early. It's so gosh darn hard telling any of the boys 'no'." He turns back to the press. "I'll be done with this in just a minute."

"You've always been gracious to a fault, Warren. I don't believe I've ever heard you say 'no' to anyone. Good thing you're not a woman. You'd be pregnant all the time. . . what on earth are you doing?"

"Tomorrow's front page. Nothing quite like typesetting to relax the mind. You cannot imagine how I miss it."

"I see. Why not get yourself a little printing press to play with while you're in Washington?"

"Matter of fact, I have. Called the United States Treasury." He smiles at her. "You look wonderful. As always. And how is Mr. Phillips?"

Carrie peers up at the wall clock. "Almost lunch time—he should be two sheets to the wind by now." She pauses. "I'd had hopes of—seeing more of you this summer."

Harding fumbles with some letters and seems to need an extra moment to respond. "Actually, I don't expect I'll be here but a week or so. Possibly you've heard—Teddy Roosevelt wants back in the White House. He's asked me if I'd pitch in and. . . "

"Of course. I can certainly understand how a prominent and distinguished United States Senator might no longer have much time for. . . "

"Now that's absolute rubbish." He stops work, wipes his hands with a towel and rises. "And as for 'prominent and distinguished,' truth is, Carrie, I'm pretty small potatoes in that place." He utters a sad little laugh. "Quite mediocre. I doubt my being there has made the slightest difference. To anyone."

Carrie stands and moves toward him. "You are anything but mediocre, good sir. And you continue to make a profound difference. Especially to me." She caresses his face. "Wherever you are." She aims her lips at his mouth—and somehow gets his cheek.

For a moment she just looks at him with a penetrating gaze, then takes a step back. "You've been seeing someone. Haven't you."

"I'm sorry?"

"Six months and what—two letters? Slip quietly into town. Don't call." Her soft, full mouth hardens into a tight smile. "You have someone. In Washington."

"No. Not—not really."

"Not really? You know, Warren, the truth doesn't hurt nearly so much as your keeping it from me."

Harding shakes his head. "We're just friends."

"'Friends.'"

"She's—quite young."

"Certain skills women pick up at a remarkably early age these days."

"Please, Carrie —. Don't. There's never been. . . there'll never be anyone. . . like you."

Carrie's eyes glisten as they sweep lovingly across Harding's face. "You're a dear sweet man, Warren," she says, softly. "I wish I could have kept what we had. I truly, truly do." She shrugs. "But I'm forever mired down here, and—you're there." She reaches out, squeezes his hand, then turns away. "I should go."

"Carrie, let's talk a bit. . . "

"Goodbye. . . Senator." She's hurries from the room, Harding following. Awkwardly, he pushes the front door open for her, jingling the bell. She flies out and down the street. Harding watches her unhappily from the doorway, takes a deep breath, and slowly exhales.

13.

The entire nation was shocked when on the 2nd of February, 1919, Teddy Roosevelt passed away. Suddenly, in his sleep. Gracious—he was only sixty-one and the very model of robust health and American vigor. Perhaps it had something to do with the terrible Spanish influenza that was going around, but who would have expected it?

It was an especially difficult loss for the Republican National Committee. Mr. Roosevelt was our leader and certain presidential candidate. There was really no one to take his place. And our annual Lincoln's Birthday Ball was but a week and a half away. I can assure you none of us were feeling very festive. But finally, the Committee decided to go forward as planned. They said Teddy always loved a good party. And they saw it as an opportunity for their wisest minds to work out who amongst them might best pick up the torch.

On the evening of February 12th, a fleet of chauffeured limousines pull up to a Washington estate on Delaware, one block from Embassy Row. Black men in white gloves scurry to open their doors. Animated passengers, many well lubricated, emerge in their gowns or tuxedos, trip up the marble steps, gold and gems glittering, and sweep into a mirrored ballroom humming with the Lodges, Falls, McPhersons, Sinclairs, and most every other Republican of note, there to be greeted by a stern, life-size portrait of Theodore Roosevelt, rimmed in black crepe, and by its side, one of Abraham Lincoln, no less sober.

Beneath the social chatter and gladhanding, a great deal of serious politicking is under way. None is more intense than that of two heretofore relatively obscure men. The first of them, three-star General Leonard Wood, ramrod straight in his full dress uniform, is visibly uncomfortable pretending to be just one of the boys, and is doubtless wishing he could simply *order* the party to give him the presidential nomination. Lobbying effortlessly across the room is the man deemed best positioned to deny the general his fondest hope, Thomas Lowden, the ambitious governor of Illinois, physically slight but brandishing an outsized political sense.

Off in a corner, Nan endures the enthusiasms of her nominal escort, a spirited young congressman who for the last twenty minutes has been pontificating upon the immorality of taxing corporations. She has positioned herself so as to always keep the ballroom entrance in view; her lecturer immediately loses what little of her interest he may have enjoyed when she spots Harding and Florence making their appearance, arm in arm, Florence leaning on a cane.

At last, my darling—the first time I'd laid eyes on him in a week—and for me, the main reason to attend the ball. Tonight, Florence, who seldom ventured out of Marion, unexpectedly chose to accompany her husband. I myself had not seen her for over a year, and I was now struck by, well, how ***old*** *she looked.*

Over her companion's shoulder, Nan's eyes follow the two new arrivals threading their way through the room. Harding's personal popularity is unmistakable as he fields a flurry of warm greetings and handshakes, surprised smiles at his wife's rare appearance, and many a manly embrace. Just as he's making a quarter turn to reach another outstretched hand, Nan catches his attention, charging the air between them. He winks at her, she giggles. Nan's congressman assumes she's enjoying his last turn of phrase and chuckles along with her, then realizes she's looking past him. He spins round and follows down her line of sight, just as Harding turns away.

Harding and Florence inch along in the general direction of the party's most seasoned hands, senators Fall, Lodge, Guthrie and Harry Daugherty. The four insiders glare at the "outsiders," Wood and Lowden, as the two scratch for commitments.

Fall shakes his head. "Will you look at that pair!"

Lodge raises his glass to Roosevelt's portrait. "After the giant dies, the pygmies emerge from the forest."

"T.R.'s body's barely cold," Guthrie grouses, "the convention months away, and already they're scrounging for votes."

"Nonentities," scoffs Fall. "Both of 'em." He turns to Lodge. "The nomination's yours for the asking, Henry. I'd bet my ranch on it."

Some twenty feet away, Harding, having deposited Florence with several other wives, starts handshaking his way towards the quartet. Daugherty spots him coming and decides the moment is at hand to launch his audacious, convoluted plan. "From what I hear, Al, you've bet your ranch once too often. And in all due respect, gentlemen, I find these two particular 'nonentities' quite worrisome." Daugherty looks squarely at Lodge. "One of them just might collect enough delegates before the convention to deny the nomination to the man we all know to be Roosevelt's rightful heir."

Lodge shrugs. "I doubt that. So they've picked up a few promises. It matters less who casts the votes than who counts them."

"Things are shaping up differently this time, Senator," maintains Daugherty. "The convention could run away from you. With Roosevelt gone it's likely to be wide open."

Though loath to admit it, Lodge is troubled by Daugherty's admonitions. "All right, assuming that it is a possibility. . . ?"

"I'd quietly start gathering in your I.O.U's. Tuck 'em away. Then, come the convention, we let Wood and Lowden have their moment."

"Their moment?" asks Lodge.

"They despise each other. That's good. We encourage 'em to fight it out. Exhaust themselves while you lie low. When it looks like they've about knocked each other off, you step in. Gather up the pieces. The only ballot we need be concerned about is the last."

"That's fine, Daugherty," interposes Guthrie, "but what if, early on, like you say, either Lowden or Wood proves stronger than we thought? Maybe even sweeps the primaries."

"Yeah," says Fall. "Suppose the *first* ballot is the last, and one of them walks off with the nomination, right out of the box?"

Harding has finally reached the four conspirators. Daugherty couldn't have timed it better. He gives Harding a big smile and places an arm around his shoulder. "That's where party loyalists come in. Loyalists like our Warren, here. For example, we have Ohio commit 'irrevocably' to Warren Harding for President."

This is news to Harding. "What on earth are you talking about, Harry?"

"As Ohio's favorite son. Merely a gesture, Warren. *But* you'd tie up all of Ohio's delegates. Keep 'em away from Wood or Lowden's people as long as necessary. That's a huge block of votes you'd have tucked there in your pocket. Then, at the propitious moment, you simply release 'em to Henry, here. And as Ohio goes, so goes the Midwest."

Harding knows full well that favorite son is a harmless holding position, not a serious candidacy, yet he is suddenly enveloped by a sinking, anxious feeling. "I don't know, Harry. I'm not sure that's such a. . . "

"Indeed," says Lodge, thoughtfully. "No Republican has ever won the presidency without Ohio. Best to keep those delegates under lock and key." He turns to Harding. "Don't look so glum, Warren. Running for the White House can be quite elevating. Be assured, years from now you'll look back on your presidential flirtation with great fondness."

14.

Florence is especially eager for this week's preview of portentous events. Sitting across from her Marion seer, she leans forward, elbows resting on the gingham tablecloth. "I trust you know—my Wurr'n will be amongst those advanced at the convention next month." The reliably clairvoyant woman facing her from the other side of the kitchen table today seems puzzled. Florence persists. "The Republican's nominating convention. In Chicago?"

The woman looks up from the cards spread out before her. "Actually, ma'am, I've never understood politics. So I don't pay much attention. I'm sorry. . . "

"He tells me he's not really a candidate," adds Florence, casually. "He says he isn't there for himself. Just helping out someone else. This other senator. Senator Lodge? Henry Cabot Lodge? A very important man in Washington."

"I don't believe I'm familiar with the gentleman. Still, quite the honor."

"Yes," says Florence in a flat voice. "Quite."

"I know how much you've given of yourself to Mr. Harding's work. By all rights, you must be feeling a great lady."

Florence shakes her head. "There are no great ladies in America. Just the occasional muffled, invisible woman—married to a great man. Hmph. Little did my father guess."

"Pardon?"

"My father—he's barely spoken to me since I married. *'Beneath my station,'* he said." A sardonic smile. "Wurr'n's 'suspicious blood lines,' you see."

"Ah. I believe I did hear something—years ago. . . "

"Then Wurr'n is elected to the U.S. Senate. *That*, father never expected." She closes her eyes. "And now this."

"A swift change of fortune," observes the woman.

"Yes. A swift change." Florence opens her eyes, hesitates, then again leans forward and whispers. "Can you tell me—what will happen? Is Wurr'n. . . could my husband actually become President of the United States?"

The woman looks down, repositions several cards, and replies slowly. "I believe that he could."

Florence takes a deep breath. "And. . . will he? *Will* he?"

The woman studies the cards' configuration, looks up at her, says nothing, again stares down. The wall clock ticks off the seconds like gun shots. "Well? What is it?"

At last, the woman nods "yes."

Florence swells with pride. "All these years I believed in him. Even when *he* didn't. Those rumors about his family—vicious nonsense."

"Yes, ma'am."

"Now Wurr'n will show them, won't he." She starts to rise.

The woman holds up her hand, rings on all five fingers. "If you please. . . wait, Mrs. Harding. Just a moment, if you would." She weighs her words. "Should your husband proceed on this course, there are—hazards. It may not be for the best."

"What—what are you saying?"

Brow furrowed, the woman searches her cards for the right words.

Florence continues in a rush. "A most extraordinary thing is about to happen. You—you've seen it yourself. Yes, certainly there'll be problems, tremendous responsibilities, difficulties to be worked out, my God, that's to be expected. But my Wurr'n, President—*'not for the best?'* What a thing to say!"

The woman looks up at Florence's flushed face—and retreats. "As I've stated, ma'am, I don't understand politics." She smiles faintly. "Often life is illusion. Much is unclear. All the cards can ever offer is a bit of guidance. Hardly infallible."

Florence stands. "Indeed not." She opens her purse. "How much do I owe?"

The woman shakes her head. "The reading was very clouded today, Mrs. Harding. No charge."

15.

Over the next six months I had dinner with Mr. Harding once a week. Right before his regular Wednesday night poker. Of course, even on my generous salary, supplemented now and again by my darling, it was no easy task coming up with that many different ensembles, but I was determined that he would never see me in the same outfit twice.

The dear gentleman would call for me at my apartment at exactly 5:45, always with some lovely gift in hand—a blouse in my favorite color (green), a charming bracelet or brooch, once he even brought a book he thought I might enjoy. I felt very much loved. In every way—but one. Then, on the first Wednesday of August, for my twenty-second birthday, he gave me a rather special present—a first-class train ticket. I was to be a page at the nominating convention in Chicago.

August 10th, 1920, with its record temperature of 106 degrees, finds the Republicans at the Chicago Coliseum, breaking a record of their own—day three, a *thirteenth* ballot, and still no nomination. In over one hundred years, no previous nominating convention of either major party has ever required more than six ballots to choose a presidential candidate. But just as Daugherty had predicted, this year's two front-runners, Wood and Lowden, whose antipathy for the Democrats pales alongside that harbored for one another, emerge from the primaries in a dead heat. Now neither seems able to close on the 497 votes required by the rules of the convention; and none of the favorite sons or wanna-be's has yet to indicate the slightest willingness to donate the several dozen votes necessary to put either of the two leaders over.

The convention floor, hot, smoky and cacophonous, is jammed cheek by jowl with nearly a thousand delegates, their aides and committee staff. Nan is everywhere amongst them, bouncing hither and yon, relaying messages. The delegates, clumped together by state, are to a man—

and they *are* all men—wilted and bone-tired. Waving above this roiling sea of damp Republicans are signs with names of the forty-eight states, posters touting the candidates, state flags and banners.

Much of the floor is about equally divided between Lowden and Wood supporters, but loyalists for Senator William Borah of Idaho, Massachusetts governor Calvin Coolidge, businessman-philanthropist Herbert Hoover, and the perennial standard-bearer, Henry Cabot Lodge, together are also substantial in number. Only the Ohio delegation totes Harding signs; few others at the convention have more than a vague idea who Warren G. Harding might be.

A large "scoreboard" of electric lightbulbs behind and above the dais flashes the candidates' names alphabetically, followed by their current delegate count:

Borah	24
Coolidge	18
Harding	33
Hoover	35
Lodge	55
Lowden	399
Wood	425

Lodge presides at the podium, aided by a hollow-sounding public address system that alternately booms, squeals, or, on occasion fades away entirely. As dicatated by protocol, none of the candidates, save Chairman Lodge, is personally in the hall, but their campaign people are spread throughout, lobbying furiously for votes, shouting with variable success to be heard over the din.

Those four extraordinary days in Chicago were among the most exhausting—and exhilarating—of my entire life. I got to witness ballot after ballot, always with the same result—deadlock. How fascinating to actually see America's democracy in action. And here was I, right in the middle of it all. I think I lost ten pounds. I doubt if I slept the whole time.

At her post by the dais as the fourteenth ballot nears completion, Nan is handed a message by Lodge's fraying but still dapper campaign manager. She then weaves her way back across the floor in the direction of the thirty-three-strong Ohio delegation to make delivery, while Lodge, through the loudspeaker, calls out the last few states. With each response, the numbers on the board shift accordingly. "Utah?"

Utah's whip responds. "Mr. Chairman, Utah casts its 18 votes for Idaho's great senator, William Edgar Borah."

"Washington?" asks Lodge.

"Washington will continue to cast its entire 24 votes for General Leonard Wood," bellows its whip.

"Wisconsin?"

"Mr. Chairman, we have 12 votes for Wood, 12 votes for Lowden, 2 votes for Hoover, 1 vote for Lodge."

The tally has changed slightly. Wood's votes have fallen to 411, again nearly even with Lowden, now holding at 410. But Dan Wicker, manager of Lowden's campaign, believing the momentum finally to be his, once more pushes through to the Ohio delegation's whip, the band on his straw boater predicting "Lowden in 1920" darkened with sweat. "Hi, Billy."

"Status quo," insists Ohio's whip.

"You know, Billy, with a mid-westerner in the White House, a lot of that Illinois gravy is going to spill over into Ohio. . . "

Yeah, yeah. Look, Dan, we all like the governor, you know that, but we're standing pat with Warren till Daugherty says 'go.'"

"The governor can't wait much longer. If Wood should finally pick up one more big state. . . "

"Ah—Wood's stuck. Goin' nowhere. Think he's topped out."

"How about releasing five—just let me have *five* delegates—give the governor a little lift. You can do that much for an old friend, can'tcha?"

Ohio's whip gives that some thought. "Maybe. Gotta ask Daugherty. You haven't seen him, have you?"

In point of fact, no one on the convention floor had seen him because Daugherty divined early on that the votes he was going to need lay elsewhere; and over the last three days, every waking moment had been consumed by the challenge of securing 497 of them for his heretofore invisible candidate.

Daugherty could never resist a speculative enterprise, though paradoxically, for much of his life, he had thought himself supremely unlucky. His adversities had begun in childhood. Raised Catholic, by the age of fifteen he understood that his sexual orientation would forever deny him the comforts of the church, and would almost certainly ensure a markedly constricted family life, to say nothing of eternal damnation.

Then, after scraping through law school, Daugherty found he had neither appetite nor aptitude for working within a legal framework, that his real talent lay in ferreting out weaknesses in codes of procedure so as to circumvent the rules that governed, or—in his view—impeded men's progress; unfortunately, this knack for obtaining special advantage also served to get him his license twice suspended for a year, and more recently brought him within a hair's breadth of indictment and disbarment.

As for financial matters, he was Midas inverse—touch gold and through some perverse alchemy it turned immediately to lead. All that a promising corporation required to precipitate bankruptcy was for Daugherty to invest heavily in its securities. He did no better in commodities; his bet on a bumper crop at the Mercantile Corn Exchange two summers past brought devastating drought followed by locusts. By contrast, the following year he single-handedly brought a bone-dry spell of some four months to an abrupt and torrential end simply by forgetting one night to put up the top of his Plymouth convertible coupe.

At the track, his horses were never in the running; the last time he went with the favorite it had thrown its jockey, then had smashed against the inside rail and broken its leg.

Having failed at everything else, his obvious course was to try for political office, only to find himself again stumbling into every pothole: in a race for city council, he managed to come in dead last in a crowded field; in a subsequent race run State Assembly, he was disqualified even before leaving the starting gate when half the signatures on his nominating petition were found to have been penned by voters who had passed on some years before.

But politics ultimately proved his salvation, for though Daugherty was utterly without vision for himself, he could perform flawlessly for others. Much like the sightless but brilliant musician who as compensation is able to master a complete repertory entirely by ear, in the last decade Daugherty had orchestrated with perfect pitch the election of several state senators and assemblymen, a lieutenant governor, two mayors, U.S. Senator William Foraker, and then, to the Democrats' astonishment and chagrin, Senator Warren G. Harding. Today he was to bring all his political perspicacity and ambition-by-proxy to bear upon this, the darkest horse, the longest odds, the most improbable and least-willing presidential candidate in the history of the White House.

At 10:05 in the morning of August 13th, Daugherty pushes into Lowden's hotel suite at the Drake, jumping and buzzing as dozens of the governor's people hustle in and out. He scans the room and after a moment spots the governor himself, working the phone, lips almost brushing the mouthpiece.

"I'm well disposed to having Coolidge on the ticket," Lowden purrs, with the confidence of a politician who has never lost an election. "How many delegates can he bring along? Not promise. *Deliver!*" The answer he hears elicits grudging approval. "Yes, all right. But Coolidge should understand that I need them *now*. Looks like Wood may be getting a second wind." He listens again and seems satisfied. "Fine. Please, get right back."

He hangs up and is surprised to see the man he's been trying to reach for the past two days standing directly in front of him. "Daugherty—when the hell are you releasing Ohio?"

"Now you know, Governor, our first commitment is to Henry. Until he's ready to make his move. . . "

"Henry's not going anywhere. Not in this convention, any more than the last convention, or the last three before that, or the next twenty. A senator he is, a senator he shall remain."

"I know, I know," concedes Daugherty. "And Ohio is certainly keenly aware that its best interests lie in the mid-west with you." It was time to roll the dice. "Tell you what. If—*when* you get right up to where Ohio's votes would kick you over the top, I'll give you everything we've got—Ohio plus a few others I've tucked away in Texas and California. I figure thirty-nine delegates all told. The moment you gotta have 'em, they're *yours*." He pauses. "But not until you're up there. You understand—no sense getting Henry all upset prematurely."

Lowden discerns that this is the best deal Daugherty can give him. "You'll guarantee that they're there when I need them? Because I will!"

"They've already got your name on them. Engraved. You have my word."

"Harry, I'm in your debt." A brisk handshake. "And you might mention to Harding that I never forget an oblig-ation."

"That is a fact, Governor, a well known fact." He pauses. "And, if I may ask? Suppose, just suppose that you can't quite get far enough. Even with our support lined up. *You* stall—begin to slip back, Wood starts picking up your defectors. . . "

"I'd never allow that military neanderthal to. . . "

"Just for discussion's sake. We stand at the ready to help you stop Wood, of course, but try as you might, you still can't make the magic 497. At last, you figure it's over. We all wish to hell it wasn't, but the worst has happened.

With or without Ohio. Wood is poised to sweep the convention." Daugherty chooses his next words with care. "Might you then release *your* people to us?"

"Release my. . . ? You mean, to *Harding*?"

Daugherty nods.

Lowden laughs. "Warren Harding?! *President of the United States*?"

Down on the convention floor, Lowden with 430 votes is fast pulling away from Wood whose delegate count has dropped to 391. None of the other candidates are showing any signs of life. Lowden appears unstoppable.

Nan glances up at the scoreboard just as Wood slips further, to 378. Harding clings to Ohio's 33—exactly where he started out three days earlier.

I was one of two dozen pages assigned to the convention. We could have used twice that number. I was on the go twelve, sometimes thirteen hours a day. Still, I didn't mind. Whenever it seemed I couldn't last on my feet another minute, I'd look up and see my darling's name in lights, and I'd feel so proud and full of energy again. I could just picture Mr. Harding hunkered down in his campaign headquarters, working away on strategy.

As Lowden is on the verge of taking the nomination, Harding's strategy is to take a nap. Alone in his "campaign headquarters," he lies on the bed of a small hotel room, jacket off, vest unbuttoned, tie loosened. He could use a shave. On the nightstand, a small electric fan blows ineffectively. The room is decorated with a single, forlorn "Warren G. Harding for President" poster.

There's a knock on the door as it opens, and Charlie Forbes enters carrying a brown paper bag. He sets it down on the table next to the phone and extracts a pint of bourbon and bag of pretzels. "I swear," says Charlie, "this town's practically out of booze. Had to hit five liquor stores to find one lousy pint. 'Old Tulip Mash.' Who the hell's ever heard of 'Old Tulip Mash?'"

Harding rouses himself, sits up, nods and stretches. "I think, pal, I'm about ready to ask Harry to release our boys. So we can all go home. What's the latest?"

Charlie shrugs. "Same. Lowden, Wood. Wood, Lowden. Still a stalemate, though Lowden's got the edge. He just might make it this time."

"Fine. Lowden it is. We've done our bit. See if you can reach Harry."

Charlie nods and picks up the phone.

But Harry Daugherty is not about to let anyone reach him—not till his mission is complete. And he now faces the most delicate and difficult leg—striking a deal with a man who doesn't deal, who sees political give and take as beneath him.

He saunters into General Wood's hotel suite, no less crowded than Lowden's but relatively quiet, orderly, and with a clear chain of command. Wood, out of uniform, looks stiffer yet in coat and tie. As Daugherty approaches he spots Coolidge's campaign manager there ahead of him, hawking his wares.

Wood's not buying. "There's no way in hell I'm going to use the selection of the man a heartbeat from the presidency as a bargaining chip," sniffs the general. He turns away dismissively.

Coolidge's man tries again. "The governor would be quite content with Secretary of Commerce. How 'bout Interior. . . "

Wood turns back to him sharply with a Medusa stare. "How about dog catcher? Tell Governor Coolidge *I don't make deals*."

"Yes, *sir*!" He leaves in a huff, shooting past Daugherty.

Clearly not the best time for Daugherty's proposition.

Unfortunately, the only time. Daugherty steps forward. "General?"

"Yes—what?" Wood does not recognize Daugherty, but then rarely does he remember civilians.

"I'm Harding's man—Harry Daugherty. Ohio's favorite son—Warren Harding? Been looking forward to seeing you again, sir."

"Ah yes, Harding. I'd thought he'd have declared for Lodge by now. Or gone over to Lowden."

"It's pretty clear neither of them is going to make it, General. We both know that." Daugherty puts a toe in the water. "Not unless a massive number of *your* delegates switch allegiance. . . "

"*My* delegates will hold the line. To the last man."

"Of course, of course. But you may never have quite enough of them. Fourteen ballots, and—forgive me, sir—you're still coming up short." Daugherty pauses, then gingerly takes the plunge. "Might you consider a modest proposal?"

"I very much doubt it."

"One I'm sure you can live with."

Wood looks at Daugherty as if he were the target at a shooting range. "Well?"

"I'll release delegates promised me in Texas and California—thirteen in all—to you. At once. And I'll keep Ohio's thirty-three *away* from Lowden."

Wood's eyes narrow. "And in return?"

Cautiously, Daugherty lays it out. "Should you and Lowden remain deadlocked, if it became clear that neither of *you* can break out —."

"Well?"

"I would ask that you think of Warren Harding."

Wood absorbs Daugherty's proposal, his face impassive. "There's not a whole lot there to think about, is there? Nothing against the man personally. . . "

"General, if *you* can't be the nominee, could you in good conscience endorse any of the others? Lowden?"

"Certainly not. He'd auction off his children for a few votes."

"I can't see your people mending fences with Lodge. . . "

"Not on his death bed. . . "

"Borah?"

"Egomaniacal windbag."

"Hoover? Coolidge. . . ?"

"All right. Point taken. So far as I'm able to tell. Your man's pretty damn quiet. . . "

"Like you, General. Warren is a quiet man. Thoughtful, unassuming—and presidential. Have we an understanding?"

But however skillful Daugherty's machinations, it may be too late. Back on the convention floor Lowden is finally about to pull it off. Flashing up above Lodge and his campaign manager, the scoreboard now gives the Illinois governor 440 votes—just a scant 51 to go. Wood has slipped, doubtless fatally, to 331. Lodge and the other impecunious hopefuls remain stalled at double digits—55 for the chairman, 35 for Hoover, a steadfast 33 for Harding, 22 for Borah, a mere 19 for Coolidge. Everything is going Lowden's way, though he is not quite secure; to achieve the summit he must still corral a last handful of delegates beyond the prospective gift from Daugherty.

Nan scurries to the podium with a Lowden envelope. Lodge's manager tears it open and reads quickly, just as Lowden's supporters begin a rhythmic chant—"*Lowden, Lowden*" —softly at first, then louder and insistent as, one by one, other delegates across the floor get caught up. Lodge's manager shakes his head. "Wood's fading, Senator. Looks like Lowden's gonna pick up some of his boys."

"Never," insists Lodge. "Any Wood delegate makes a move toward Lowden, he'd face a firing squad."

"Henry, the delegates have been at this three days! It's 150 degrees in here. They just want to choose someone, *any*one, and get the hell home. It's going to be Lowden. The next ballot."

“Mm. We’ll see.” He flips on the microphone, and his voice reverberates throughout the hall, drowning out the chanting. “*Ladies and gentlemen. The Chair calls a brief recess.*”

The whole of the Illinois delegation and several hundred other enraged Lowden supporters respond with cries of “No!” “Fraud!”

Lodge is unmoved. He whacks his gavel and stomps off.

16.

In their hotel room a few blocks from the coliseum, Harding and Charlie Forbes concentrate on gin rummy, indifferent to the crisis on the convention floor, to them a world away. They have but two discernible problems—they've been unable to locate Daugherty so as to officially pull Harding's hat out of the ring, and they've polished off the last of the liquor.

Charlie slips a watch from his vest pocket and checks the time. "I'll try down there again." He picks up the phone, dials, listens for a moment and shakes his head. "Tuh. Still busy."

Harding stands and heads for the bathroom. "Well, pal, I'm tired of hanging around up here, missing all the fun. I'm going to pop in there, personally track down Harry, and tell him to pack it in. Then say hello to some old friends. I believe Al Fall's on the floor somewhere." He smiles. "And a certain young lady."

"Hey, aren't you supposed to wait till you get the nomination—*then* make your triumphant entrance?"

Harding stands at the sink and wets his shaving brush. He chuckles. "Get the nomination. Sure. That's exactly what I'm gonna do, too. President Harding. The same day palm trees bloom in Siberia." He lathers up.

In a dimly lit corner of the convention hall, Lodge and his manager are going through the motions with deal makers for both Hoover and Coolidge. Lodge conjures up a final bit of bravado. "Don't bother releasing me your people when I'm breaking 400. I won't remember your names."

The two aides do their best to look cowed, nod and depart just as Daugherty approaches. Lodge turns to him. "Daugherty—where the hell have you been?"

"Just sitting tight, Senator."

"Well time to get off your kiester. I'm going to stop Lowden. Ohio ready to go?"

Daugherty doesn't bat an eye. "Ohio is all yours, sir. Just been waiting for your nod."

"I'm cashing in." They start for the convention floor. "And Daugherty—tell Warren I owe him."

Flushed by the heat and a still impressive level of blood alcohol, Harding strolls the five blocks from his hotel to the convention hall. Off in the distance, a clock strikes midnight, its chime muffled in the muggy air. Arriving at the coliseum, Harding attempts the front entrance, only to be stopped by a security guard.

"See your delegate's badge, sir?" asks the guard.

"Well," replies Harding, "you see, I'm not a delegate, but actually, I'm sort of a. . . "

"Sorry, sir. No badge, can't letcha in. Got strict orders."

Harding nods goodnaturedly. "That's okay. Say, what's the latest?"

"I hear Lowden's 'bout got it wrapped up."

"So it *is* Lowden, after all." Harding shrugs affably. "He's an able man. Should do fine. Too bad about Henry, though."

"Henry?"

"Oh—a friend of mine. He was thinking things might turn out differently."

Harding nods and wanders away, just as two delegates arrive, flash their badges, and are promptly admitted. They saunter through the convention foyer past a bank of phone booths, each occupied by a reporter rattling off copy. One of them, H. L. Mencken of the *Baltimore Sun*, though just at the early edge of his fame, already carries great weight with the other newsmen.

"Lowden remains way out front," dictates Mencken into the receiver, cigar cocked out of the side of his mouth. "But he still can't break 440. So near and yet so far. Meanwhile, Wood continues to slip. . . "

Mencken's protégé, a cub reporter covering his first convention, is working the adjacent booth. ". . . bottom fishing for any odd delegate. Lodge finally showing some movement. . . "

Simultaneously, on the convention floor one flight above, an unprecedented *fifteenth* ballot is in progress as Lodge, his self-serving scheme in motion, finds himself presiding over a last false hope for his near half-century of presidential ambitions.

"New Hampshire?" he asks.

The New Hampshire whip hollers back. "New Hampshire is proud to cast its 16 votes for Henry Cabot Lodge."

"About time," mutters Lodge. "New Mexico?"

"New Mexico casts 12 votes for Lowden, 2 for Lodge," replies New Mexico's whip in a Western drawl.

So much for Albert Fall's sworn promises. But Lodge is heartened to see that with all but two of Harding's delegates now his, and some North Atlantic states showing interest, he's gathered up a respectable eighty-five votes and climbing, while Wood has faded to two hundred and twenty-eight. Most encouraging, Lowden has abruptly tumbled to three hundred and fifty-five, down from four hundred and forty just two hours earlier. Perhaps this time, this time. . .

From her perch on a wooden folding chair, an exhausted Nan looks up at the numbers.

My worst moment came, I think, with the fifteenth ballot. Mr. Harding had suddenly lost most of his delegates. It seemed his own state had abandoned him. But as they say, it's always darkest before the dawn.

In Marion, Ohio, a hundred and eighty miles to the east, Florence Harding sits propped up in bed, eyes closed, seemingly asleep as Dr. Sawyer makes an adjustment to the medical apparatus near her feet, then picks up his black bag and slips out of the room.

Florence opens her eyes. She takes a Bible from her night stand, quickly finds a passage, and begins to pray. A light breeze through a half-open window toys with the curtain.

It is now nearly 2:00 A.M. in Chicago. Most of the windows of the hotel housing Wood's campaign headquarters are dark. But those of Wood's suite on the twelfth floor remain brightly lit. The general's workers sit around drinking coffee and smoking, having simply run out of ways to try to staunch their candidate's hemorrhage. Wood keeps busy working the phone. "Surrender" is not part of his lexicon.

There's a stir in the outer room. Wood is startled to see Lowden and a small entourage stride in. He cuts his call short. "We'll talk again later."

"Morning, General," says Lowden.

"Good morning," replies Wood, stiffly, putting down the phone. There's no effort on either part to shake hands.

"Is there a place we can talk?" asks Lowden.

"I conduct my affairs in the open, sir, not behind a tree. I'm no politician."

"Indeed, General. And if I may say so, you've small hope of becoming one. Unless we join forces."

"Join forces?"

Lowden nods. "I'm offering you a place on the winning ticket." He pauses. "A Lowden-Wood ticket."

Wood stares at him. "You want me as *your* Vice-President?" "

Lowden nods again.

Wood smiles contemptuously. "I'd sooner be Sheriff of Nottingham."

Outside and just around the corner, Harding looks through the plate glass window of the Dearborn Bar & Grill and is pleased to find a lively late-night crowd. He strolls in, unaware that this ordinary, casual act permitted every American of legal age is shortly one he will never again be free to enjoy.

But Nan is at the coliseum to bear witness.

The moment is buried indelibly in my memory: I was perched on my folding chair off in a corner of the convention floor, giving my poor feet a bit of relief, when I sensed that something was different. All at once the hall seemed strangely quiet and there was a sort of tension in the air. I looked up at the scoreboard. Suddenly it was as if my heart was too large for my chest—before my very eyes, Mr. Harding's numbers shot from 2 to 74 and then to 94! Without even waiting for a formal ballot, several entire states had come over to him. I confess to this day I've no idea what great issues Mr. Harding had staked his candidacy on but his strategy clearly had begun to bear fruit at last.

Nan is hardly the only one startled by this turn of events. Up at the podium, Lodge confers disconcertedly with his manager, then flips on the microphone. "The Chair moves that the convention adjourn till tomorrow morning, ten o'clock." A querulous murmur ripples through the hall. Lodge continues. "Those in favor signify by saying 'aye.'"

A few tired *"AYES."*

"Those opposed?" Lodge asks perfunctorily.

A great thunder of *"NO'S."*

No matter. Lodge whacks his gavel. "The ayes have it. This convention is adjourned till 10:00 A.M." Pandemonium throughout, rage amongst Lowden's people, but Lodge turns coolly from the podium and heads for the exit, whisking past Nan.

Though I'd always known my darling's remarkable abilities would tell in the end, few party leaders expected it, I think. Oh that I were privy to their thoughts and to their surprise and delight in Mr. Harding's achievement, as this long, long convention entered the home stretch.

Lodge and his senatorial clique, with Daugherty trailing along behind, reach the ground floor foyer and sweep past reporters working the telephone bank. The dutiful journalists who for three stifling days have perfunctorily rattled off the same copy again and again, glassy-eyed with boredom, unable to find fresh ways to describe an intractable Republican stalemate, now are galvanized into a body of alert heralds who perceive that they are witnessing history.

Mencken continues to monopolize the first phone booth, firing the emerging story off the top of his head. ". . . front runners still deadlocked on this, the nineteenth ballot. But dark horse Warren Harding, an innocuous man known primarily for his sonorous platitudes, inexplicably showing dramatic signs of life. There is speculation on the floor that the exhausted delegates have no place else to turn. Moments ago, the powers that be unexpectedly called a recess, so something. . . "

On the adjacent phone, the cub reporter is losing his voice. ". . . Harding," he rasps. "Warren Harding! *Warren.* Coming out of nowhere." He listens for a moment. "That's right, *Harding.*" He listens again. "I tell you I've tried. Nobody here knows much about him." He listens. "Right. Nothing good but nothing bad, either. What am I supposed to do, make something up. . . ?"

A reporter for the *Chicago Tribune* is further plagued by a poor connection. "Harding!" he shouts. "*H-a-r-d-i-n-g.* The senator from Ohio. Ohio. *O-H-I-O.* Look, that's all I—hang on a minute. . . "

All of them drop their phones and turn their attention to Lodge as he and his brain trust race by.

"Senator. . . ?"

"Would you care to make a statement . . .?"

"Is Harding. . . ?"

But Lodge, with a backward wave of his hand, fobs them off on Daugherty, and is out the door. Daugherty smiles as the press converges on him, pens poised.

Mencken is given the first shot. He aims for the heart of the matter. "So it's all gonna be decided at 3:00 A.M. in a smoke-filled room, huh, Harry?"

"Make it 3:11, Mr. Mencken," Daugherty replies with a wink. "Yes, 3:11. Actually, gentlemen, here's how I see things shaping up. First off, as you doubtless have all observed. . . "

While Daugherty is dallying with reporters, the object of their intense interest, the man at the eye of the developing storm, has found safe harbor in the Dearborn Bar & Grill—Harding has not only gotten his hands on the first truly decent bourbon of the night, he's spotted a high stakes poker game underway at a far corner table. And he's feeling lucky. Enormously lucky.

But a far larger gamble is to be played out in Lodge's campaign suite—spacious, well-appointed and generously supplied with cases of Mumms and "President Henry Cabot Lodge" banners. Lodge has spared no expense, fully expecting that at last he would be his party's nominee. After close to fifty years of faithful service, who was more deserving?

The candidate, his manager and six key senators stride in, continue through to a smaller room, and close the door. As they settle into chairs and light their cigars, Lodge prepares them for what just twenty-four hours ago—*three* hours ago—would have been unimaginable.

"Time to face facts," he tells them. "Lowden and Wood are finished. Both of them."

"Good riddance," adds Senator Guthrie.

"Regrettably," continues Lodge in a flat voice, "the grass roots support we anticipated for *our* candidacy seems . . . not to have materialized."

Lodge's manager strives for a silver lining. "Nor for anyone else. Hoover's stuck."

Senator Paxton joins in. "Coolidge and Borah are burned out. . . "

"It appears," says Lodge, resigned to the celestially improbable, "that the only man still on his feet. . . is Warren Harding." He pauses for deliberate effect. "Gentlemen, we'd best ride the horse in the direction it's going."

Lodge's manager is the first to catch his boss' drift. "Harding? You're not serious, Henry."

Lodge looks at him steadily but says nothing. For a long moment the room is still. A shroud of melancholia settles heavily upon the men.

Morris Webb breaks the funereal silence. "Well, why not Harding?"

"Why *not*?" asks one senator, indignantly. "He's a born follower."

"The man wants only to be liked," observes another. "Touching in a spaniel. . . "

Webb persists. "Warren's always been there when any of us needed him."

Webb is bombarded from every side as the senators erupt. "So has the Senate barber," comes a salvo from across the room. "Why don't we just nominate *him*. . . ?"

"God knows Harding's congenial, but he has no passion," another senator insists.

"I don't think the fellow's even been to college, has he? Admittedly, he's reasonably well-spoken, but. . . "

"He never actually *says* anything. I can't recall his ever taking a firm stand. On any issue. Can you?"

"Scratch Warren's surface and you come out the other side. . . "

"Christ, Henry," grouses Lodge's manager, "there isn't a man in this room who isn't infinitely more qualified for the presidency than Harding!"

Vigorous nods of agreement, the odd "here, here."

Lodge remains unmoved. "What's most important, Senators, is that Harding *is* one of us. And after eight years of Woodrow Wilson, the *Senate* deserves a President—a President who'll see things *our* way."

The men quietly chew on that as the room clouds with cigar smoke. You could hear an ash drop.

Finally, Albert Fall speaks up. "Face it, friends," he says, softly. The delegates are at the end of their string. If we don't all line up behind someone, someone *now*, they'll bolt. Stampede to Coolidge. . . "

"They could even give it to Hoover, God forbid," mutters Blair. "After Wilson, the one thing this country doesn't need is another do-gooder in the White House."

Webb weighs in again. "Warren's already drawn more delegates than Hoover and Coolidge together. He might pull it off, gentlemen. He very well might. If *we* get out the word."

Lodge has reserved his most potent arguments for last. "Senators, consider: Warren Harding seems nearly incapable of alienating anyone. Given the voters' current mood, that alone makes him eminently electable. And of greatest importance, *Warren Harding is one man who listens to his betters*."

Harding's betters look at each other and prepare to bite the bullet. Lodge rises from his chair. "Then we're agreed?"

A collective sigh through the room. Paxton shrugs. "As they say, Henry: in America *anyone* can become president."

Harding has settled in comfortably with a half-dozen new friends around the Dearborn's poker table, cracking jokes and winning one pot after another. An attractive flapper in a short skirt stands close by, admiring both the man and his enormous pile of chips. The dealer calls. Triumphantly, Harding shows his hand. Everything is going his way.

At the coliseum, for the last time in his long political life, Lodge holds down his party's convention podium; though not yet a quarter-way through this, the twenty-first ballot, the early numbers already make clear to him and almost everyone else that the protracted nominating convention of 1920 is coming to its astonishing and utterly unforeseen end:

Borah	18
Coolidge	6
Harding	188
Hoover	35
Lodge	46
Lowden	165
Wood	130

Across the floor, Nan watches mesmerized as Harding's numbers climb.

"The sunshine state of Florida," intones its whip, "casts its 24 votes for Harding."

"Georgia?" asks Lodge.

"The state of Georgia gives 4 votes to Wood, 18 votes to Harding, 4 votes to Lowden."

Up in Lowden's suite, Lowden's manager, Dan Wicker, has his ear to the phone, his eyes trained on Lowden, waiting for guidance. Tight-lipped, Lowden nods "yes."

Lodge continues his march through the states. "Illinois?"

Unhappy turmoil amongst the Illinois delegation. Lowden, after all, is their governor.

Lodge tries again. "*Illinois*?"

"Illinois casts 4 votes for Lowden," comes the answer in a hoarse voice. There's a pause. Then a new voice, loud and clear: "42 for Harding."

A murmur ripples across the convention floor.

Lodge plugs away. "Iowa?"

"Iowa casts its 16 votes for Warren Harding."

Harding's thrust now appears irresistible. Though more than a few delegates are too tired to care, the Ohio contingent starts to chant:

"Harding! Harding!"

Slowly, Nan rises from of her chair to stand with her gaze fixed upon the scoreboard as Harding soars and the others fade away.

At 4:00 A.M., Harding closes down the Dearborn and staggers out onto the street. He passes a hideously scarred, blinded veteran leaning against the wall, selling pencils. A hand-lettered sign propped up on a small table reads: "GASSED IN 1918." Sobered somewhat by the vet's disfigurement, Harding reaches into a pocket, pulls out a good chunk of his winnings and stuffs them into the man's tin cup, shakes his head sadly and continues on.

Simultaneously, Maine's whip, who had just cast 17 votes for Harding and 8 for Lowden, interrupts himself. "Excuse me, Mr. Chairman. Correction—that's 2 for Lowden, *23* for Harding." The impact of this revision rumbles through the convention hall.

"God help these great United States," mutters Lodge, as he moves on to Minnesota.

"Minnesota casts all 31 votes for Warren Harding."

One Minnesota delegate turns to another. "Who the hell is this guy?"

"Hey," comes the response, "I just do what I'm told."

The Republican's moment of truth has come. "Pennsylvania?" Lodge asks. Despite the microphone, his voice is increasingly submerged by chants of "Harding! Harding!"

Pennsylvania's whip rises portentously. "Pennsylvania. . . is proud. . . to cast the entirety of its 54 votes. . . for our next President. . . *Warren Gamaliel Harding!*"

Harding is over the top.

Nan stands rooted to the ground, her curls matted down with perspiration, Harding's flashing score of 510 reflecting off her shining face. Around her, from floor to ceiling, the convention reverberates with yells and cries, perhaps more of relief than of joy.

Lodge struggles to make himself heard. "The Chair moves that the nomination be unanimous. All in favor?!"

"AYES" come roaring back at him, all but smothering a distinct number of loud *"NO'S"* from Lowden and Wood diehards.

“The Chair declares, by unanimous acclaim: Warren G. Harding is the Republican nominee for the Presidency of the United States!”

As hundreds of straw boaters are tossed into the cheer-saturated air, Lodge slams the convention gavel. Then he lays it down on the podium, removes his spectacles, pinches the bridge of his nose and slowly shakes his head. He feels quite old.

At that precise moment, the newly-anointed candidate is wandering into the Blackstone Hotel, drawn by a curious sight: a half-dozen late-night patrons sit at the lobby bar, enjoying a nightcap or sipping cups of coffee—but all wearing headphones. At either end of the room, signs tout “*The wonders of wireless. Hear the news of the day the day of the news.*”

Harding takes a stool. The bartender approaches. “What’ll it be, sir?”

“Bourbon, pal. Straight up.”

The bartender shakes his head. “‘Fraid we’re out of bourbon—between the politicians and the press. Got a little gin.”

“Sure, that’ll do,” says Harding, amiably. He picks up a spare headset. “This radio thing is somethin’. What’s everyone listening to?”

“They’re broadcasting from right down the street,” replies the bartender. “Coliseum. The Republican fellas? Seems they finally got together. Picked their man. Sure took ‘em long enough.”

“Yeah,” chuckles Harding. “I heard. Lowden.”

“Nope, wasn’t him.”

Surprised, Harding looks at him. “Wood?”

The bartender shakes his head. “This guy I never heard of. They spend four whole days huffing and puffing, then choose some nobody.” He leaves Harding his gin.

Harding’s going to need it. He puts on the headphones.

17.

The convention floor continues its clamor for a man no one knows. Or seems able to locate. Nan, long a student of Harding's habits, edges past the Ohio delegation in time to see Daugherty lift Charlie Forbes off the ground by the lapels. Jess Smith observes Charlie's plight with some satisfaction.

"*A walk?*" shouts Daugherty. "Probably the next frigging President of the United States—you let him go out for *a walk*? In *Chicago*?"

He drops Charlie and turns on Jess. "Call the goddamn room again."

"Just did, chief. No answer."

Daugherty shakes his head. "Jesus, Mary and Joseph. All right. Grab Burns, anyone else you need, start with the bars, then the bordellos. No—not you, Charlie. I want *you* to. . . "

Nan slips away.

Minutes later she scurries down the hall of Harding's hotel, reaches Harding's door and knocks softly. No answer. She knocks harder. The door cracks open. Cautiously, she pushes in.

Harding sits on the edge of the bed, alone in semi-darkness. She goes to him.

"They've given you the nomination, Mr. Harding." Harding doesn't respond. "I guess you heard," Nan continues.

Still no response.

She kneels down and takes his hand. "Perhaps you ought to go to them now. Say a few words." She pauses. "May I be the first to offer my congratulations."

Finally Harding speaks. "I'm going to do my best. I'll try not to let them down." He's still a little drunk.

"You've never let anybody down. Not in your entire life."

"I'm an ordinary man, dearie. Just an ordinary man. But how can I say no?"

"Of course," replies Nan, gently. "You can't." She caresses the top of his hand.

"I let them put my name in," says Harding. Now *I've* got to see it through.

"I know."

"Good God, Nan. What if I win? I could, you know. It's possible."

She reaches out, strokes his cheek. "You'll be the best President the country's ever known. . . "

"This Democrat Cox—plenty bright, but tied to Wilson. The People—they've had enough of Wilson. Christ—they just might vote for me."

"They will. Oh, I know they will. And come to love you. As I do."

Harding turns to her. He can barely discern her silhouette in the darkness, but at that moment remembers her face as the loveliest he has ever known. "You really do, don't you. You really do. Lord knows why." He kisses her once, gently.

"I always trust my heart," explains Nan. "That's why."

She kisses him back. He responds, then pulls away.

"Nan, I have to tell you. . . "

"Perhaps you could tell me later," she says, again moving towards him.

"In the Senate there's ninety-six of us. Nan, there's only *one* President. All eyes will be on him. And anyone close to him." He sighs. "I don't want to lose you."

"No, never, ever —"

Another kiss.

"I think," says Harding softly, "that you might be the only person in my entire life who's never asked something of me. No, you never have, have you. Not a gosh darn thing."

"You give me everything. Just by. . . being here. With me."

Back on the convention floor the delegates, punchy with fatigue, continue their rhythmic chant in a single voice:

"*Hard*ing. . . ! *Hard*ing. . . !"

Burns wearily returns to Daugherty. "I've got half of Chicago's finest out searching for him. Don't know what else to do."

Daugherty points to the exit. "You're a detective, aren't you? Get the hell out there and do some detecting!"

Burns need only to have looked in Nan's arms.

Harding kisses her ears, her neck. "I don't want to lose you, Nan. I don't want to ever have to give you up." Another kiss. "Not for the White House, not for any. . . "

"You'll always have me, Warren." Open mouthed, she kisses him on the lips. "You're all that matters to me. You."

They're into each other deeply now, hands searching hungrily, clothes pulling off.

Harding buries his face in her breasts. "Don't want to lose you. . . "

While in the convention hall, the delegates chant:

"*Hard*ing! *Hard*ing!"

Harding and Nan envelop each other on the carpeted hotel room floor. He enters her.

"Never give you up, Nan."

"You have me. For ever and ever. Oh lord in heaven, you have me. . . "

18.

And so, for one magical, brief fragment of a single night, Mr. Harding had been mine, entirely mine. Yet even at that exalted moment, I knew that I would have to quickly step back into the shadows again and let him go, that all too soon I would be sharing him with the entire country.

An apricot dawn is breaking over the coliseum as Harding and Nan hurry to the entrance of the convention hall. She shows the security guard her pass. He waves them through.

The floor is thinning out as the exhausted delegates, resigned to Harding's inexplicable reluctance to show himself, torpidly pack it in. Harding, still utterly unrecognized, stands with Nan at the rear of the hall. He gives her hand a loving squeeze. They look at each other. Then, as if in a dream, he slowly begins the long walk alone towards the podium.

Gradual awareness, beginning with those nearest Harding, spreads across the hall in an expanding wave. Delegates stare and point. Several reach out to shake his hand, others pat him on the shoulder. Those further away clamber up on chairs and tables to glimpse a man few outside Washington or Marion have ever seen. Albert Fall catches his eye and gives him the high sign. And then the chant of *Harding! Harding!* starts to boil up again as the delegates crowd around the anonymous man in whom they have placed their faith, hoist him on their shoulders, and bear him towards the podium.

Nan, all but invisible at the pageant's periphery, watches her lover's triumph with a beatific smile as tears roll down her cheeks.

PART THREE

19.

I saw my darling just once more back in Washington—an idyllic afternoon we spent together in my little apartment—before he was totally enveloped by the folds of his campaign. As you may imagine, he was greatly concerned about the enormity of what he had taken on. Nevertheless, he said that if it was truly Warren Harding that they wanted, he would just have to try and somehow do the job. But had he anything to offer, he asked himself repeatedly. Which of his ideas, if any, were worthy of an entire nation?

Then, after weeks of worry, it came to him—that America was "merely Marion, Ohio, writ large," he said. That wherever in the country they might live, people were just people, sharing common hopes and dreams. That he would simply be talking to folks every bit like himself. And I must tell you, from then on, his speeches became a symphony.

Decked in red, white and blue bunting, the plush Baltimore & Ohio pullman that conveys presidential candidate Harding back to Marion to open his campaign is a quantum leap from the drab day coach in which Senator Harding had quietly left Washington for the Chicago convention just a week earlier. Daugherty has planned the prodigal son's return with the same attention to detail he'd employed to manipulate his nomination, today marshaling hundreds of enthusiasts, some shipped in from as far away as Cleveland, to receive the candidate at Marion's train depot. To follow is a "pre-victory parade" to the Harding home on Oak Street, the route fortified with a massing of Harding placards, banners, and cheering supporters that would rival any Potemkin village.

But first, about a mile out of town, the train slips off to a siding to collect Florence. From there it slowly backs the remaining distance to the station so that the initial glimpse Marion has of its now most celebrated citizen is that of him and his adoring wife, arm in arm, waving at them from the platform of the caboose. The sea of people milling about the station platform parts as it might for Moses, as the Hardings descend from the train and make their way through their well-wishers to an open Packard phaeton, where Daugherty and Jess Smith wait, chauffeur Bobbie Burns behind the wheel. Minutes later, Burns shifts up through the gears and wrestles the ponderous motorcar around a corner and on to Oak.

Harding stands up in back and tips his hat right and left to rooters lining the road. He is surprised and flattered to find each and every fence, tree, and building in either direction bristling with flags and plastered with life-sized posters of his own face—save for Carrie Phillips' house—shuttered and conspicuously unadorned.

This one short drive from the train station proves to be the extent of Harding's travels for the duration of the campaign. Daugherty has decided to keep the candidate close to home, cheered by the warm and familiar, and shielded from overly close press scrutiny. Let Harding's Democratic opponents, James Cox and his young, energetic running mate, Franklin Roosevelt, exhaust themselves tearing about the country. For Harding the country could come to Marion.

And come it does. Over the next month Harding will stand on his front porch facing groups of some several hundred, a remarkably large number of them dewey-eyed women, all crammed onto the small lawn listening attentively as the candidate disgorges an oration he will repeat with few changes from that very spot, day after day.

By week's end, he no longer needs notes as his rich baritone rings out over the assembly. "You and I, we all want the same things for the country, don't we," asks Harding, rhetorically.

"Yes, sir," and "We sure do," come the replies.

"We all want to see Washington return to *normalcy*—it is not heroism that this great land now needs right now, but *healing*. Not new foreign adventures but a return to uniquely American virtues, to an old-fashioned patriotism, to the cherished values of the small town—my small town, your small town, our parents' small town. A return to an uncorrupted rural America, with its purity of spirit. That spirit, my friends, is America's very soul." A great ovation adds to Harding's growing confidence.

Daugherty and Jess Smith have been standing to the side, gauging audience response. Jess turns quizzically to Daugherty. "'America's very soul?' The hell's he talking about, Harry?"

Daugherty shrugs. "Just listen to how it *sounds*. I'd sure wanna vote for him." He points a finger at the enraptured crowd. "And so, dear Jess, do each and every one of them, God bless 'em."

One week before the election, in the early hours of the morning of November 2nd, Bobbie Burns turns his supercharged, sunrise-yellow Stutz roadster off Cleveland's Fourteenth Street and into an alley behind a decrepit two-story wooden building in a run-down section of the city's oldest industrial district. Daugherty had several times expressed his "concerns" about a certain publisher of "scurrilous tracts" whose presses were located there. That was enough for Burns. He didn't need it in writing.

Burns drops the Stutz into neutral, kills the engine and waits several minutes, occasionally glancing up and down the narrow passageway. Satisfied that he's alone, he slides a can of kerosene and a paper bag stuffed with oily rags off the seat next to him and brings them along as he steps down from the car and approaches the rear of the building. The sky is moonless, the nearest visible electric light blocks away.

He rattles the back door. Locked. He pulls a rag at random from his collection, wraps it around his fist and punches out a small window pane, reaches inside, unfastens the catch on the sash, and slides the window up. He drops his incendiaries, then himself, inside.

Flipping on a flashlight, Burns finds himself surrounded by printing presses and book-binding equipment. Moving to the room adjacent, he quickly comes upon the object of his visit—stacks of books and political monographs —*The Coming Aryan Revolution, Racial Pollution In America,* and most particularly, *Warren Harding, The Negro Candidate.* Burns chuckles at the last title as he unscrews the cap of the fuel can and sloshes kerosene about, taking care to saturate the Harding tract, scatters his rags into the puddles of kerosene, strikes a match and sets them ablaze. He watches for a moment as small fires become bigger ones, then reach out to one another to form a solid wall of flame.

As Burns turns away from his handiwork, a light comes on in the makeshift bedroom above, where Professor Esterbrook Chancellor, Ph.D. in anthropology, implacable white supremacist, and publisher of Purity Press, is awakened by the smell of smoke. Clad in shorts and socks, he bounds down the stairs and bursts into the press room just as Burns is about to climb back out the window.

"What the devil. . . ?" Chancellor sputters, and impulsively charges at Burns. Unperturbed, Burns holds his ground as if waiting for a softball pitch, then slams his flashlight hard against his oncoming attacker's head and clubs him to the floor. Nonchalantly, he returns to the window and scrambles out.

By the time Burns tools his roadster out of the alley back onto Fourteenth Street, Dr. Chancellor and his publishing enterprise are engulfed by fire.

20.

As we all know, 1920 was a watershed year: Prohibition became law and ladies got the vote. Perhaps we were no longer allowed to drink, but women could at last pick whomever they most wanted in Washington to look after their interests. For us, the choice was very nearly unanimous. And so it was that handsome Warren G. Harding, the love of my life, became the twenty-ninth President of the United States. The women of America had been able to discern what I had known since childhood—that a great, kindly, humble man walked amongst us. For me, that was intoxicant enough.

On inauguration day, Harding and the outgoing President, a gaunt, mortified Woodrow Wilson, ride side by side towards the Capitol Building in the open, presidential Pierce-Arrow. Wilson, his hair snow-white, his left side palsied, looks twice Harding's age, though at sixty-two he is in fact just seven years his senior. His silk top hat is as threadbare as he. Harding wears his, sparkling new, at a rakish angle.

Wilson, the most literate man since Jefferson and the most eloquent since Lincoln to sit in the White House, is today as much ravaged by profound disenchantment with the electorate—and a bitter disdain for the President-Elect—as by his recent stroke. Harding does his best with Wilson's arctic silence, turning to his stricken companion with the warmest of smiles.

"Florence was most appreciative of Mrs. Wilson's finding the time to show her through the White House."

Wilson remains silent.

"Sure need lots of help to keep *that* place going."

Nothing from Wilson.

"Back in Marion, Florence always insisted on doing everything herself."

Wilson nods. Encouraged, Harding tries once more. "Boy, some motorcar, these new Pierce-Arrows. Hard to tell this buggy's moving, the ride's so smooth. . . "

Wilson finally speaks. "Purely an illusion, Mr. Harding. Be assured: the road ahead is one of potholes, ditches and rocks."

Harding contemplates that for a moment. "Well whatever the hazards, I plan to follow your example, Mr. President—always to do what's *right* for the country."

"As should be obvious from my example, sir," replies Wilson icily, "doing what's *right* for the country is a prescription for humiliation."

They arrive at the foot of the Capitol steps. From the Pierce-Arrow they appear endless and perilously steep. A Secret Service man opens a rear door. Wilson looks up at the formidable staircase with apprehension—grasps his cane with a tremulous hand and struggles to lift himself out.

Harding is alarmed. "Mr. President, would you mind if we, er, continued on to the back entrance? Only a handful of steps there—a far easier climb for us both. I have a mighty strenuous day ahead of me."

Wilson is much relieved—and touched by Harding's tact. He speaks to the chauffeur. "Starling, Mr. Harding's suggestion is most sensible. Please take us to the rear." He nods at the Secret Service, the door closes and the two Presidents continue on. For the first time, Wilson looks directly at Harding. "Most gracious of you, sir. The Senate's thrown me down once. I wouldn't care to fall a second time." There are tears in the proud man's eyes.

Minutes later, at the top of the Capitol steps, Harding, with Florence incandescent by his side, is sworn in by a rotund William Howard Taft, now Chief Justice. Familiar faces are amongst those privileged to be within shouting distance of the new President—Dr. Sawyer; Senators Lodge, Webb, Guthrie, Paxton and Blair; and the gang of four, Harry Daugherty, Jess Smith, Al Fall, and Charlie Forbes, already instinctively drawing together. This last quartet of men, surrounded and tantalized their entire lives by the limitless wealth and unbridled power of others, themselves now face a future of infinite opportunity.

Obscured by his position behind and off to the side of

President-Elect Harding, Fall slips a piece of paper to Jess Smith, who glances at it and passes it on surreptitiously to Daugherty. Daugherty examines it for a moment, smiles to himself, then tucks it in his pocket.

Nan, crowded in amongst the masses below, looks up in rapture as Harding turns to the microphone and begins his inaugural address. But neither Daugherty, Smith, Fall, nor Forbes will hear a word of it. Their thoughts are elsewhere.

No President had ever before been swept into office on so high a tide of affection and hope. Yet as we were to later discover, even on that first day of brightest promise the evil termites had already begun their terrible work, chewing at the very foundations of my darling's presidency, so as to destroy it. Although I could not then have even imagined it, unprecedented treachery and corruption were soon to follow.

PART FOUR

21.

Mr. Harding's finding ways for us to steal a little time alone together was challenging enough during the campaign. Now that he was actually President of the United States, our situation became impossible. It was as if I were again that forlorn teenage girl living back in Marion, limited just to seeing my darling's cherished face in the newspapers. But I resolved to be patient, for I understood that those critical first few weeks in office are when a determined leader is preoccupied with grasping the reins of government, marshaling his troops, and taking command.

French windows, slightly ajar, open out to an expanse of green running five hundred yards from the White House to Pennsylvania Avenue. It is 1921 and sheep still mow the lawn.

The new President pauses in the doorway of the Oval Office. Gingerly, he slips inside and over to his desk, stacked high with letters, many more of which spill out of mail sacks piled on an adjacent table. He runs his fingers reverently along the gleaming walnut, then turns and with slow steps circles the room, pausing to gaze up at successive portraits of Washington, Jefferson, Lincoln, and lastly, of Theodore Roosevelt in his rough rider uniform. He touches one of Roosevelt's boots. "Damn big," he murmurs.

The office door opens with a knock and Mrs. Samson, Harding's new personal secretary, hand-picked by Florence from the White House pool, shows herself in. The most mannish of women, a factor doubtless weighing heavily with the Duchess, she demonstrates the aptness of her name as she effortlessly manhandles another fifty pound mail sack towards Harding's desk. "*More* office-seekers?" Harding asks, as he hurries to lift the sack from Mrs. Samson's formidable arms and add it to the others.

"Afraid so, Mr. President. And this batch is mostly Democrats."

"Democrats?"

"Yes, sir. They all claim they switched and voted for you. You'll see. And your first appointment is here, sir."

Harding brightens. "Have him come in, Mrs. Samson, have him come in."

As if on cue, Dr. Sawyer appears in the doorway and enters as Mrs. Samson withdraws. "Mr. President, I presume?"

"Don't give me any of that 'Mr. President' crap you old son of a gun. Come on and sit down. I'd offer you a bourbon but Wilson either didn't drink or took all the booze with him. Now with Prohibition, the Secret Service tells me they can't just pop out and get. . . "

"I'm fine, Warren. Christ, it's eight in the morning. How long have you been up?"

"A while," Harding replies, "quite a while." They both sit. Sawyer looks up at the cadre of previous tenants staring down at them. "Yeah, Doc—I keep wondering what the hell *I'm* doin' here with that bunch."

"I'll bet every new President felt that way," says Sawyer. "You'll be getting lots of help, I'm sure."

"Maybe. God knows I'm going to need it. Especially from folks I can count on." Harding pauses. "Folks like you."

Sawyer beams. "That's swell of you to say, Warren. Don't know what I can do exactly, but you should always feel free to. . . "

"Doc, I'd like to appoint you Surgeon General."

"Whazat?"

"I need a Surgeon General, Doctor Sawyer. I'm offering you the job."

Sawyer looks at him in astonishment. "Warren, I'm just a country doctor. An *old* country doctor. . . "

"I don't want some paper-shuffling bureaucrat. I want a real medical man. I'd like you to try and do for all Americans what—well—what you've done for Florence. Whad'ya say? Will you help me out on this?"

"I, I. . . "

"This way you'd be here in the White House, keeping a

close eye on the Duchess. She won't let anybody else treat her anyway. Says Washington doctors are all society quacks."

"Jesus, Warren, what in hell do I know about running a—a. . . ?"

"I'll bet every new Surgeon General felt that way." He smiles. "I need you, Doc. Give it a try? For Florence's sake."

Sawyer peers unseeing for several long moments at the sheep grazing just outside the window before he answers. "If that's what you want—Mr. President."

"I do, Doc. Gotta have a few familiar faces around. Friendly faces." He shakes his head. "My pals from the Senate have invited themselves over this morning. Wanna give me a little 'advice' on my cabinet appointments."

"Hell—you're President of the United States now, Warren. Once in a while you can actually tell someone '*no*.'"

"*No*?" Lodge bellows, nearly apoplectic. "What do you mean '*no*'— Mr. President?" Now it is Lodge who finds himself at the far and deferential foot of a long table, ringed with some mighty unhappy senators.

Harding presides at its head, and struggles to make his case. "Henry, I want—I need to surround myself with the best minds this country has to offer. Men with the experience, the—the education I don't have. Scholars who. . . "

"Scholars?" snarls Lodge. "Woodrow Wilson was a scholar. A *Princeton* scholar. What a disaster. . . "

"And Harry Daugherty?" asks Blair. "Some scholar."

Guthrie nods contemptuously. "Some 'best mind.'"

"Look, boys," says Harding, "I've depended on Harry since I came to Washington. This is one hell of a job. Didn't want it. But I'm stuck with it. I'm gonna need Harry's help. I asked him how he thought he could best serve. He told me."

"But," sputters Blair, "*Attorney General*?!"

"Harry's a lawyer," says Harding, "and he's clever in all the ways I'm not."

Morris Webb smiles ruefully. "That's what worries me."

Guthrie looks down at the list in his hand. "All right—Al Fall at Interior—now *there's* a solid choice, but in all due respect, sir, why *Herbert Hoover*? And Secretary of Commerce, no less."

"Two months," Blair asserts, "and he'll have the country's economy dismantled. . . "

"Gentlemen," says Harding, evenly. "Might I be permitted to point out we're talking here about the *President's* cabinet. Not the *Senate's*."

This simple statement of the obvious only pours fuel on Blair's fire. "It was the *Senate* that put you in the White House, Warren. We all cashed in a lot of chips. . . "

"Called in favors," adds Paxton.

"Gosh. I thought the people of America put me in the White House. And what we owe *them* is nothing less than the best."

With that, Harding seems to silence all of them—save Lodge. "I believe, sir, there's a difference of opinion here as to just who might be 'the best.' May I remind you—Mr. President—that each and every one of these appointments of yours is going to require Senate confirmation." Nods and murmurs of agreement circulate around the table. "Now I can live with Daugherty and with your nominees for some of these lesser posts, but if you want *any* names to get through the Senate, at a minimum you're going to have to take Hughes for State and Mellon for Treasury. There are two scholars for you. The *right kind* of scholars."

More nods, more murmurs.

Morris Webb tries to take some of the sting out of Lodge's ultimatum. "Accommodate us a bit here, Warren, we accommodate you a bit there. Give us something today, we give you something tomorrow. You know how these things work."

"Oh yes, Morris," says Harding with resignation. "I know how these things work. I surely do."

Two days later, Jess Smith and Bobby Burns, both wearing ill-concealed smirks, sit in the last row of a federal courtroom, watching Harry Daugherty place his right hand on a book he's not touched since childhood. Miraculously, a lightning bolt fails to materialize, and God leaves him undisturbed to swear fidelity to the constitution of the United States, the President, the laws of the land, and the people of America. Then accompanied by his two cronies, Daugherty leaves the room as U.S. Attorney General.

Right off the bat, my darling found that even a President has to battle tooth and nail for everything he wants. And battle he did. While Mr. Harding accepted the Senate's advice on some of his cabinet choices, like Mr. Hughes and Mr. Mellon, he insisted on appointing one of his closest associates, Mr. Daugherty, to run the Justice Department.

Across the hall in a small federal hearing room, Charlie Forbes stands before a clerk, hand over his heart.

He also made sure to find a place for his old friend, Charlie Forbes, putting him in charge of Veterans' Affairs. (I don't believe Mr. Forbes was ever a veteran, exactly, but he ***had*** *spent time with the Ohio National Guard.)*

And no matter how crowded his official calendar, Mr. Harding made sure to have one hour set aside, six afternoons a week, every week, just for his "saying hello" to The People—ordinary people who came to see the White House and who might also want to meet him. It was ***their*** *White House, after all, and he was* ***their*** *President. He said that they had every right to look the guy over and shake his hand if they wished. It was a marvelous thing, I think, for a President to do. But I must confess,* ***something*** *felt a little unfair—total strangers were free to visit with my darling, when I could not.*

Monday afternoon a radiant President Harding strides out on the White House lawn to greet a couple of dozen boy scouts. Each gets a handshake and an encouraging pat on the shoulder.

On Tuesday, with Secret Servicemen on their mettle in the background, Harding wades into a mixed group of delighted tourists who can't quite believe and have no idea why they're shaking hands with the President of the United States.

On Wednesday, this time with Florence by his side, he stands in the Rose Garden, beaming broadly as he hands out flowers to a Brownie troop.

On Thursday, accompanied by the new Secretary of Interior, Albert Fall, he welcomes a disoriented group of Native Americans in full Indian dress. Fall slaps the chief on the back. "Just call me Al," Fall says to the chief.

On Friday, Harding gets to clown with Charlie Chaplin in his Little Tramp persona, and shake hands with Al Jolson in black face.

And, on Saturday, joined by Charlie Forbes, his Director of Veterans' Affairs, Harding greets a group of disabled young veterans in the company of their Red Cross nurses. Most of the men are missing an arm or leg, or are in some other way disfigured. Harding is moved by this grievous evidence of the Great War's carnage, his eyes glistening behind his smile. One of the men unselfconsciously offers Harding the stump of his wrist. Without hesitation, Harding grasps and shakes it warmly.

Spending time with The People each afternoon was one part of the President's job my darling really enjoyed. Perhaps the only part. As for the rest—he found much of it pretty rough going. Especially his cabinet meetings. Thank the good Lord he had some of the country's finest intellects to advise him.

Presiding over his weekly cabinet meeting, Harding does his best to follow what is becoming a running debate between his nineteenth-century Secretary of Commerce, Herbert Hoover, and his eighteenth-century Secretary of the

Treasury, Andrew Mellon. Harry Daugherty, Charlie Forbes, Secretary of State Charles Evans Hughes, Admiral Todd Denby of the Navy Department, Albert Fall and several other appointees listen as well—with varying degrees of attentiveness. Invariably, Vice President Calvin Coolidge sits stiffly upright—and is sound asleep.

Where Hoover is doggedly well-meaning, Mellon is simply mean; like most Treasury Secretaries of this nascent Republican decade, Mellon husbands a personal fortune the rival of that overseen in his official capacity, and has no plans to share the smallest portion, least of all with the federal government.

This week it is Hoover who has started the argument. "If we lower import tariffs, Mr. President, then raise upper bracket income tax proportionately to make up for the revenues lost, prices will come down and increase both goods and money in circulation." Sounds reasonable to Harding, who nods in agreement. Hoover is encouraged. "I'm convinced that this would equalize wealth somewhat, and greatly expand the country's economy. . . "

Secretary Mellon stirs. A gaunt, desiccated man, he has a parched rattle of a voice—like rats in the pantry. "I'm afraid, Mr. Hoover, you're advising the President to take the first pernicious step from capitalism to socialism."

Harding frowns and feels tugged the other way. "We certainly would never want to do *that*. Um, kindly tell us all again, Mr. Mellon, as you see it, the principal difference as might apply here between the two?"

"Certainly, Mr. President. In a word, capitalism is a cruel economic system wherein one is either very well off or wretchedly poor. Socialism would replace that with a fair and equitable system—wherein *everyone* is wretchedly poor."

"I see," says Harding. He needs a tiebreaker, and turns to his Secretary of State, distinguished academician and former president of Columbia University. If anyone held a monopoly on unbiased truth, surely it would be he. "What is your view of the matter, Mr. Hughes?"

Hughes takes several leisurely puffs on his pipe before speaking. "From State's perspective," he intones, "both arguments have merit. Equal merit." He returns to his pipe.

"Uh huh," says Harding. His eyes dart around the room, finally coming to rest on Daugherty, pencil in hand, furiously editing some papers. "See any legal implications, Harry?"

Startled, Daugherty looks up. "Ah, Justice has no position, Mr. President."

"I see," says Harding.

All eyes are on the President. The seconds tick by. Mellon waits with the patience of a man holding long-term securities. Hughes puffs. Daugherty scribbles. Coolidge sleeps.

Hoover breaks the silence. "Might I ask your decision, Mr. President?"

"Gentlemen," says Harding, "this is your area of expertise. You two settle it, figure out how we could best handle things. Maybe split the difference. Whatever you decide, I'll back you up."

Hoover and Mellon look at each other.

"Well," Harding continues, "anything else?"

They've all had more than enough. Except for Daugherty. "It would expedite the new Veterans' Hospital contracts, Mr. President, if we could have an executive order."

"Of course, Harry, of course."

Daugherty gives the nod to Charlie Forbes who has the appropriate documents ready to go. He gathers them up and passes them over for Harding's signature.

With the country's business completed, only Harding and Charlie Forbes remain in the cabinet room. Charlie reminisces about the time he tried years ago to teach Harding how to drive and Harding had promptly crashed Charlie's Fliver into a haystack. They share a good laugh. Then Charlie heads out the door, signed executive order in hand. He almost collides with Dr. Sawyer, bizarrely resplendent in his white and gold surgeon general's uniform. "'Scuse me, Doc. Hey, that's one swell outfit. Ever need any extra gold buttons, I can get 'em cheap." Charlie gives him a mock salute and continues down the hall.

Sawyer enters the cabinet room and shuts the door behind him. "Never much cared for traveling salesmen," he grumbles. "Particularly that one." Then he takes a close look at Harding. His old friend has dropped his smile and appears drawn, tired, every bit his fifty-six years. "Warren—Christ, what's the matter?"

"Ah, I'm okay, Doc," says Harding, wearily. "Only there's so much I don't know. And I'm discovering 'great minds' cancel each other out." He flops down heavily in the chair just vacated by Charlie. "Last week Mellon gave me *his* book on economics—he wrote the darn thing, ya see. So this week Hoover gives me the economics book that *he* wrote. Both mighty big books. Several pounds each, I'll bet."

"Economics, huh? Whose made the most sense?"

Harding shakes his head. "Can't get through either one. The more goddamn pages I read, the longer the goddamn book gets. And Mellon says one thing, Hoover says the opposite." He sighs. "This is a terrible job." He pulls himself up from the chair. "Let's get out of here."

Sawyer pats Harding on the shoulder as they pass from the cabinet room into the corridor outside. "Might be easier, Warren, if you didn't charge at it twenty-five hours a day, eight days a week."

"Hell, I don't mind putting in the time, Doc. It's the least I can do. Just that I feel. . . I'll tell ya. . . I feel so. . . isolated. *Surrounded* by people."

Two White House aides, Travis and Blake, nod deferentially as they scurry past. "Mr. President."

"Mr. Travis, Mr. Blake," responds Harding. When they're out of ear shot, he shakes his head. "So much attention I can hardly take a dump in private. Yet I'm—I'm lonely, Doc. Never get to see my old pals, any more.

Everyone in this place is so damn solemn. Florence tries to be cheery but, well you know, she's never exactly been the cheery sort."

"Emm. And your—lovely young friend?"

Harding stops, turns directly to Sawyer and confides softly. "Last time—*two* months ago. For maybe six seconds. Along with about fifty other people. 'Good afternoon, Mr. President.' 'Good afternoon, Miss Britton.' I got to shake her hand. That was it."

Sawyer nods sympathetically as they resume their steps. "You know what I think might lift your spirits? Put back that old bounce? Some of these new fangled vitamins they've come up with."

"Vitamins?"

"That's what they're called. 'A,' 'B,' 'C,' 'D.' Especially 'B.' Yeah, that's the ticket, I'll bet. Regular shots—once, maybe twice a week."

"Vitamin shots. You really think that's gonna help?"

"I'm sure of it. We can have the nurse come right to your office. The sooner the better."

Sawyer makes good on his prescription the very next morning. At ten o'clock sharp, a uniformed nurse arrives at Mrs. Samson's desk, carrying a small black bag. Samson stands, walks the young woman to the door of the Oval Office, and knocks.

Harding opens the door and breaks into a big smile as Nan, in white from cap to shoes, strides in. He quickly closes the door, pulls her to him and kisses her forehead. "Look at you—my alabaster angel."

"Yes, Mr. President, I'm an angel. Today I've come to take you to heaven."

The first kiss unleashes a torrent of others, wherever Harding can find bare skin—her face, neck, hands and wrists. "I've missed you beyond words, dear Nan, dear, dearest Nan. I've been so alone. . . "

He fumbles at the pearl buttons of her uniform. She

clasps his hands in hers. "Wait—wait. Let me. . . " Nan takes a few steps back, and beginning with the first button, slowly undresses. "Yesterday I saw a Greta Garbo movie. About Mata Hari."

Doctor Sawyer saved my life. Weren't for him, I can't bear to think of what might have happened. I was wasting away, down to a hundred pounds. Could hardly sleep. And when I did, I'd have the most disturbing, terribly impure dreams. Dreams about our President. Then one day, there I was, actually walking into my darling's arms. And it was no dream. God bless Doctor Sawyer. I realize now he was one of the very few real friends the President had.

22.

In full uniform, Surgeon General Sawyer climbs the steps to the Bethesda Veterans Administration Hospital and makes his way through a shabby chronic care ward crowded with the wheelchairs of young, maimed and limbless vets, and tight row upon row of beds occupied by middle-aged and elderly men, desolate survivors of earlier and forgotten wars, most unkempt, drowsing, a few smoking; though only partially disabled, all appear lifeless. A single attendant flits amongst them, going through the motions of providing care.

Sawyer has not been inside an institution like this since his training forty years ago at a public charity hospital, where doctors-to-be had the opportunity to make their inevitable mistakes and get off cheaply. Charity patients were grateful for any sort of medical attention and were quite forgiving of the earnest young men in white who were clearly struggling to do their best. It was in those early years that Sawyer caught his first glimpse of a profound discovery he was then to see confirmed again and again in his four decades of clinical practice: Some of his colleagues were healers. Many more were not.

It wasn't just a question of smarts or diligence but of talent. An innate gift. Were a doctor not so blessed, then he might study at the finest institutions, acquire all manner of surgical skills or be the very embodiment of medical knowledge—and his patients would still do poorly. But a healer invariably saw things other diagnosticians missed. He'd discern that peculiarly sweet breath of the inexplicably feverish teenager, and thus recognize diphtheria. He could see past the white pallor of the perplexing, anemic patient's hemoglobin-starved skin, and detect its underlying subtle lemon tinge that meant not blood loss, but a pernicious vitamin deficiency. If the physician were a healer, then his very presence, his mere laying on of the hands would generate vitality and hope, energizing his patient's innate, bodily defenses. And so, most of his patients would recover.

Sawyer certainly did what he could to keep pace with medical progress, but the field was becoming ever more technical, the journals written in an increasingly arcane language he could not grasp. Yet his patients continued to do well while those of his younger, more scientific peers, often succumbed. Whatever his limitations—and Sawyer understood that these were legion—he knew that he was, indeed, a healer.

As Sawyer squeezes between beds, searching for a particular patient, he notes with anger the clinical neglect, the paint peeling off the walls and ceilings, the broken windows patched with tape. At last, in a darkened room set aside for those with inoperable cancer, he finds the man he's come to see.

Zachary Cartwright, friend to both Sawyer and Harding over the course of their long years together in Marion, is now thin, tremulous and frail—almost lost in his bed clothes. His battered, tottering nightstand boasts the only bright spot on the entire ward—a basket of fruit wrapped in yellow cellophane.

Sawyer maneuvers around two veterans in wheelchairs to stand by the head of his old neighbor's bed. "Hey—Zach. Zach Cartwright," he calls out, gently.

Cartwright has difficulty focusing, finally recognizes Sawyer, and breaks into the semblance of a smile. "Doc—I never expected. . . "

Sawyer grips Cartwright's trembling hand. "Now I *said* I was coming." He sits down on the bed, absently fingers a torn dirty sheet, but admires the fruit basket. "You seem to have a fan."

"Actually," says Cartwright in a hoarse voice, "it's from the President. From Warren. Can you believe that?"

"I can. That's Warren for ya, isn't it. So—how're ya doin'?"

"Best as can be expected. Not coughing so much this week. Boy, will you look at you! Hey—maybe you shouldn't sit there. Get your whites all dirty."

"How often do they change the linen around here?"

"Mm. . . don't really know, Doc. Lying here, one day blends into another. Not even sure what month it is. I know I've been here a spell."

"A single day would be an awfully long time in this place, Zach." He makes a fist. "And I mean to do something about it."

The hospital's medical director, in a long white coat, scoots out his office door, Sawyer nearly prodding him from behind. Together they stride down a hospital corridor as the director deflects Sawyer's anger with his own.

"I requisition paint, window glass, bedding, whatever," he explains. "Every week, asking for something. Months go by. Patients come and go, many needing bandages and medicines we just don't have. Some die."

The two men round a corner.

"And then," he continues, "we'll get these huge shipments. Buckets of paint, boxes of gauze, pharmaceuticals, new linens and blankets."

They reach their destination. The director unlocks and opens the storeroom door, swats a light switch. A single naked bulb hanging from the ceiling glows dimly. Save for two broken folding chairs, the cavernous room is empty. The director shakes his head. "Damn thing is, less than a week later, before we can hardly get to use it, most of it's gone."

"Gone?" asks Sawyer.

"We get this fool order from the Veterans Administration. Says it's been declared 'surplus.' 'Out of date.' *'Absolutely not to use.'* They'll be sending us new stuff." He waves his arm at the barren storeroom. "But first all this has to be crated and picked up. They come take it away and we start waiting again. I've phoned, written—what's his name, Forbes, Charlie Forbes—it's still screwed up." He flips off the light and slams the door. "Can't you people in Washington get anything right?"

The following day, Sawyer, now in civilian dress, enters Washington's largest Army/Navy Surplus Store, located at 300 K Street, and starts to walk the aisles, inspecting merchandise, from toothbrushes to teacups. He's not there more than a minute before coming upon a wall-to-ceiling stack of paint cans, all clearly stenciled "Bethesda V.A." Turning down an adjacent aisle, he runs across piles of blankets, linens, and towels marked "Veterans' Hospitals," all first-quality, all brand-new.

It appears to Sawyer that Charlie Forbes, the consummate peddler, is still very much in sales.

Less than a fifteen-minute walk away, at 1625 K Street, Jess Smith has set up a shop of his own in a small, two-story wooden Victorian painted bright green. The Stars and Stripes fly from a flagpole on the front lawn as they might outside any government building. A rat darts down the pole and scurries across the grass.

Inside, what had been a family's parlor has become Jess' office, its four walls papered with photographs—a large, tinted stock portrait of Harding; several photos of Jess and Daugherty; two of Harding and Daugherty with Jess hovering nearby; and one of Jess alone, feet planted on the steps of the Capitol Building as if they were his personal property.

Jess himself is on the phone, legs up on the desk, while a well-dressed supplicant, Luther Brockmann, sits across, patiently waiting for him to finish. Bobby Burns, his chauffeur's uniform retired in favor of a three-piece suit, sits off in a corner smoking a cigarette, listening to Jess' half of the conversation with amusement. Occasionally Burns pops an aspirin out of a small bottle and into his mouth, crunching down on it like candy.

"I'm real sorry," says Jess into the receiver with persuasive sincerity. "You were never supposed to be raided." He listens. “Hey, ‘at’s an honest mistake. Whiskey stills look pretty much alike, you know.” He listens. “Yeah, the Attorney General understands you produce sacramental spirits.” He looks at Burns and shrugs. “Uh-huh, the President appreciated the bourbon—yeah, *both* cases.” He winks at Burns. “You have my solemn promise.” He listens and nods. “*Yes*. Bye.” He hangs up and addresses Burns. “First I’ve heard of sacramental bourbon.” With relish, he makes a notation in his ledger book as he turns back to Brockmann. “Okay, where were we?”

Brockmann has a German accent. “I believe I was explaining, sir: my factory never made weaponry during the war—we merely supplied Germany with bicycle parts. And we are primarily Swiss owned.”

“Yeah, I see.”

“I myself am Swiss. On my mother’s side.”

Jess nods, scribbles a name and number on a piece of paper and hands it to Brockmann. “Handles all alien property for the Attorney General. Call ‘im—tomorrow. Should have Mr. Daugherty’s final okay by then.”

“Thank you, sir. You’re helping to correct a grave injustice. No one in my family has ever been pro-German or . . . ”

“Sure, Luther, I know.” He rises. Brockmann follows suit. They shake hands. “One thing,” says Jess. “Mr. Daugherty wanted me to ask—once we get your company back in your hands, about how much would, say, a thousand shares be worth?”

“A thousand shares—I’d need some time to convert stock prices into post-war currency —.” In the corner of the room, Burns shifts in his chair, somehow imbuing this slight movement with menace. “But I’ll attend to it at once,” Brockmann continues quickly. “And please assure the Attorney General that I would deem their value quite modest when compared to the generous assistance given me today.”

“Hey look,” asserts Jess, “America is the land of opportunity.”

“Ah, indeed,” agrees Brockmann. “Well, good day, sir.” He turns to Burns. “Mr. Director.”

Burns waves magnanimously, Brockmann leaves well-satisfied, and Jess nods with smiling contentment as he makes another hugely profitable notation in his swelling ledger. No longer reconciled to playing second fiddle to Harry Daugherty, he has found his own way of making music. Jess had no idea it would be this easy.

23.

In his second year as President, I saw a definite change in Mr. Harding. He was studying all manner of incredibly difficult books and journals. Sometimes he even invited their authors to the White House to explain things he might not have fully understood. He initiated friendships with other heads of state, men of different color and of greatly varied beliefs, several traveling halfway around the world to meet with him. And instead of always trying to accommodate everyone else, more and more he came up with plans of his own. Often he'd sound them out on me first. I thought they were all wonderful; increasingly, he was learning to trust his heart.

Hoover, with the rest of the cabinet in tow, meanders toward their meeting room. Just as he reaches the door, it opens, and Hoover is startled as a slightly disheveled Nurse Britton hurries out.

Minutes later a rejuvenated, assertive Harding is on his feet, pitching ideas at his cabinet with newfound enthusiasm. "Say the White House invites all the great powers to Washington. Have them sit down together. Once we get everybody in the same room, we work out a way for each to disarm. Seriously disarm. First off, we formally renounce war. . . "

"Renounce war?" exclaims Admiral Denby.

"Then find some formula whereby we all slash our navies. What purpose do these enormous fleets serve now? Let's cut 'em back. I'm talking real disarmament here, not just another dead scrap of paper. Have you any idea, Admiral, how much it costs the taxpayers to keep just one of your battleships afloat? And for what!"

Hughes puts down his pipe. "I take it, sir, you're proposing that each country scuttle some ships."

"Exactly, Mr. Secretary. Stop building all these new ones, and sink the excess we already have."

Denby is astounded. "Sink our own ships?!"

"Admiral, this is 1922—no country's about to start some overseas adventure without a huge navy to back it up."

Fall's eyes narrow with interest, but he says nothing. Coolidge slumbers on. Harding has struck a responsive chord in Hoover, however, who nods enthusiastically. "The President makes a persuasive argument. Standing armies always melt away once a war concludes. But battleships and the like go on forever. Along with their capacity for mischief. I'm certainly with you on this, sir."

Hoover's support ensures Mellon's opposition. "So," he says in acid tones, "we send half our navy to the bottom, then get everyone to shake hands and promise to be peaceful and live happily ever after. . . "

"The point," insists Harding, "is that we'll be doing away with some of the *means* to fight. No big navies, no big foreign wars."

"Sink our own ships?!" repeats Denby, several beats behind.

"Obviously," continues Harding, "we'll have to work out country by country how many. . . "

"You know," cautions Hughes, "when Lodge gets wind of this idea of yours, he'll blow the dome right off the Capitol Building. And he won't need any dreadnoughts to do it, either. He keeps a lot of those very ships you want to do away with anchored in Boston Harbor. I believe he built his home on a hill overlooking the bay just so he could keep an eye on them."

"I'll speak to Henry," says Harding.

This is all too much for Denby. "Excuse me, Mr. President, but do you really believe you can persuade France and Britain and Japan or whoever to scrap huge chunks of their *own* navies?"

"Why not?" asks Hoover. "If the United States sets an example, and everybody does it at the same time. . . "

"Right," says Harding. "And should some country breaks its pledge, we haul 'em into World Court."

"World Court?" asks Hughes. "What World Court?"
"Well, that's my next proposal, gentlemen. . . "

1922 saw Mr. Harding make another significant innovation—he began taking regular trips out of the White House, sometimes even sneaking me along with him. Previous Presidents had rarely traveled far from Washington, but ***this*** *President wanted to carry his new ideas right to the source of the problem, whether or not they liked what he had to say. So, for instance, he spoke to the Chamber of Commerce about shortening the twelve-hour day for children. I must say, not much enthusiasm there for* ***that*** *proposal.*

He went to Atlanta and talked about equal rights for Negroes. This time he got lots of applause. At least from about half the assembly—that half confined to the back.

But his most heartfelt—and certainly his most ambitious goal, was to find ways to help all the peoples of the world live together in peace. He was absolutely determined to talk the great powers into getting rid of a big chunk of their navies. He spent days and days working on his plan. He said it would be the centerpiece of his administration.

Harding huddles over a War Department table with Hughes, Admiral Denby and several naval attachés. Albert Fall wanders in and stands inconspicuously off to the side, saying nothing, but for a man charged with stewardship of the country's interior, seems uncommonly interested in naval affairs.

Every square inch of wall is papered with diagrams, each that of a country's capital ships—one chart for the United States, another for Britain, for France, Japan, Italy, and so on, down to Togoland's navy of a single cruiser last reliably sighted afloat in 1914.

Harding is increasingly exasperated. "Can someone explain to me what in hell the British and French want with all those battleships anyway? Damn war's been over for four years."

"Primarily to help govern their far-flung colonies," Hughes explains. "As you know, Mr. President, they control possessions in Africa, South America, Asia. . . "

"Seems to me," asserts Harding, "every people has a right to be governed by their own bastards. If we're gonna manage without twelve battleships, so can they." He points to a squadron of huge Japanese ships. "Now what's all these, Admiral?"

Denby, whose rise to pre-eminence has been viewed by at least a few as a direct challenge to basic Darwinian principles, stares uncomprehending at silhouettes of Japanese flattops, their shapes new and unfamiliar. An aide comes to his rescue.

"Just Japanese transports, sir," the aide says, dismissively.

"Transports," repeats Harding.

Hughes provides explanation. "Yes sir. The Japanese seem quite an agreeable lot. Courteous. Accommodating. Not like our European allies. They'll give up almost all their old battleships and cruisers, if we just let them retain their transports."

Harding turns back to Denby. "Admiral?"

"I think we could go along with them on that, Mr. President. Transports are very slow. Lightly armed." He shrugs. "All they do is carry equipment."

"Mm. What kind of equipment?"

As Denby fumbles for an answer, his aide once again fills in. "Er, aeroplanes, primarily. Yes, I believe they're aircraft carriers, sir."

A second naval attaché backs up the first. "That's correct. Their only use is to shuttle a bunch of dinky little Japanese bi-planes around the Pacific."

Denby chuckles. "Glorified freighters, really. Hardly a threat, Mr. President."

The meeting ended, Fall and Denby walk down the corridor together. Fall has learned to speak to Denby very slowly, leaving the admiral persuaded that here was one civilian cabinet member who actually talked sense.

"I guess with the fleet to be cut in half," Fall smoothly observes, "all those navy oil reserves of yours are something of an albatross."

Denby nods. "It's the biggest damn nuisance trying to run a naval base in Teapot Dome, Wyoming—twelve hundred miles from the nearest ocean."

"We could take them Wyoming oil fields off your hands, if you like," suggests Fall, magnanimously.

"Off my hands?"

"Why not? We just bring Teapot Dome back to my department. Where it belongs. Interior."

Denby nods thoughtfully. Seems perfectly reasonable. "Well, Mr. Secretary, if it wouldn't be too much bother —"

Fall slaps Denby on the back. "That's what the Secretary of Interior is paid to do, you know. Conserve America's natural resources. In the unlikely event war breaks out, the petroleum will be sitting there for you, safe and sound. I'll have one of my people draw up the interdepartmental transfer. Oh—and Admiral? Why don'tcha call me Al."

Behind his desk at 1625 K Street, Jess Smith is overseeing a little transfer of his own. He attempts nonchalance as his latest pigeon, Tim Tyler, nervously counts off a stack of five-hundred dollar bills. Faces of Harding and Daugherty smile down at the transaction.

But unexpected problems pop up in every business, however well connected. There's a commotion just outside the door as a very angry Sicilian bursts free of Burns' efforts to restrain him, and crashes into the room, Burns on his heels.

"You crooked bastard! I oughtta break-a your. . . !"

Burns grabs the Sicilian before he can throw himself on Jess. "Easy now," counsels Burns, his hands firmly gripping the interloper's shoulders.

"What in hell's happened, Marco?" asks Jess, his light tenor up an octave.

"What's *happened?* I been indicted. Seventeen violations of da Volstead Act."

Tim Tyler, his congenital nervousness greatly enhanced by this interruption, eyes his money anxiously. "I could come back later, Mr. Smith."

"Hold on, Timmy," says Jess. "Look, Marco—these high-profile cases, the Justice Department has to follow certain procedures. As does the Bureau, isn't that right, Mr. Burns?"

Burns nods.

The Sicilian looks shocked. "'Burns.' *You're* head of da F.B.I.?"

Burns nods again.

"You sons of bitches busted up my still!"

Tim Tyler stands. "I think I'm going to go."

"Timmy, *sit*!" commands Burns. Timmy sits. Jess returns to the bootlegging problem. "It's just a formality, Marco."

"Formality. . . ?!"

"The Attorney General has *no* interest in an actual prosecution. You'll see. When you come up for trial. . . "

"*Trial*? You sell me dis ten thousand dollar insurance policy. You tell me it's guaranteed. I don't quibble about price, I don't-a negotiate. I just cough up da dough. So what happens is I get arrested, I get indicted, my brewery's all smashed up by Burns here and his boys, now you fuckers are telling me. . . !"

"Hey Marco, will you calm yourself? Please. Believe me. This trial is strictly show. You gotta trust me on this."

Tim Tyler scoops up his money and edges toward the exit.

"Smart move, fella," says the Sicilian. "'Cause these guys are fuckin' whores. First they take-a your money, and *then* you're gonna get screwed."

Tim Tyler's out the door like a scalded dog, along with Jess' deal of the week.

But Jess' involvement with the Sicilian is just beginning.

PART FIVE

24.

One of the curious things I learned about Washington is that it grants each new President a sort of "honeymoon"—even his bitterest opponents leave him be when he's first starting out, and almost everybody says they want him to succeed in whatever he's trying to do. But eventually the grumbling returns. Enemies accumulate. Before long it's politics as usual, and they're all ganging up on him.

Fortunately, President Harding was so much admired that his honeymoon lasted a lot longer than most. And of course he always went that extra mile not to ruffle anyone's feathers, even those individuals he strenuously disagreed with. You couldn't help but love a man like that. But as his third year in office approached, I'm sorry to say, the lines were drawn. Attacks on him had begun in earnest. And they took their toll.

Harding, his hair distinctly grayer than when he took office, sits at his desk, now cluttered with stacks of position papers, legislation, proposals, fat reference tomes, documents and briefs of every kind—and a generous breakfast tray, neglected save for the coffee. He's reading three things at once, making notes, struggling to sort it all out.

As the clock chimes 8:00 A.M., there's a knock and Mrs. Samson enters, carrying more papers. She closes the door behind her.

"Good morning, Mr. President."

"Morning, Betsy."

"Senator Lodge is here, sir."

"God, he's prompt," observes Harding, without pleasure.

"And your schedule for today." She hands him a list of appointments.

He looks it over. "Hmm. . . any of these urgent?"

"I believe all of them, sir. Mr. President, you've hardly touched your breakfast. Shall I have something fresh sent up for you and the senator?"

"Not hungry. And Lodge doesn't eat breakfast. In fact,

I've never seen him eat. I think he's an entirely self-contained unit. Er, tea—he does like tea. Have Wally bring up a pot. And ask the senator to come in, please."

"Yes sir. Er, if you have a moment—Secretary Fall asked if you could sign these this morning."

She hands him a sheaf of documents. Harding thumbs through them with little comprehension. "What are they—'Teapot Dome' —? 'Surplus oil —?'"

"Secretary Fall says he's worked out all the details for you with Mr. Daugherty and Admiral Denby. Just need your signature."

Harding scribbles his name. "God bless Al Fall. That man carries his own weight and then some." He hands the papers back to her.

"Yes sir. Secretary Fall seems to work almost as hard as you, Mr. President. I've heard from security he's in his office past midnight sometimes. I'll collect the senator . . . "

"Thank you, Betsy."

She's just barely opened the door when Lodge fairly bursts into the room. "Er, Senator Lodge, sir," says Samson, startled, then withdraws.

"Good morning, Warren," says Lodge with even less warmth than usual.

"Good to see you, Henry." He rises to shake hands. "It's been entirely too long." He points to a chair. "Please—"

Lodge makes his own choice of seat, and wastes no time on ceremony. "Mr. President: the Senate, that is, the Party, and many of our most important constituents. . . "

"You mean contributors. . . "

"There's consternation *everywhere* about the direction you appear to be taking."

"Really," says Harding, mildly.

"To begin with, your proposed naval cuts would leave us virtually defenseless."

"Not in a world where nations sit down man to man and work out their differences. . . "

"Bosh," says Lodge. "That's a fairy tale, sir. A fairy tale."

"I'm sorry you think that, Henry."

"Well I do think that, Mr. President, I do. And I'm hardly the only one." Lodge removes his monocle and begins to polish it obsessively with a handkerchief. This is a quarrel he might have had with Woodrow Wilson—had the two been on speaking terms— but certainly not with the man he had come to imagine as his having personally groomed to be Wilson's successor.

Harding waits, allowing Lodge's agitation to subside. When Lodge speaks again, it is more in sorrow than anger.

"You know, he says, pensively, "I turned seventy-eight last week. *Seventy-eight.* Suppose I've just about run the course." He sighs. "Each year voices seem more indistinct. My eyes dimmer. Seems I'm forever misplacing things." Ruefully, he shakes his head. "I keep five fountain pens lying around now so that I can lay my hands on at least one when I need it. The world is fast fading away from me, Warren. But I'd come to have expectations of *you,* sir. High expectations that you would grow into the presidency, and pick up the torch."

"Thank you, Henry. I do appreciate. . . "

"Only to find that you've totally lost your moorings. 'Disarmament.' 'World Court.' Inflammatory speeches about 'Worker's rights.' 'Negro equality.'" Another sad shake of his head. "Fine notions, perhaps, in the abstract. But in the real world, they're prescriptions for anarchy. Look at Russia. Mexico. Hell, look at Italy. . . "

"Henry, as much as anyone I know, you've always been ready to personally lend a helping hand to those less fortunate. . . "

"Of course. I know where my duty lies. And for those same reasons of duty, this nation has established great charitable trusts. For reasons of duty, Gladys and I freely donate thousands of dollars. . . "

"But suppose it were possible to get beyond individual charity, to change the entire system a bit—so people were less likely to get into a jam in the first place. . . "

"There you go, Warren," says Lodge, his bile again rising, "sounding like a goddamn Bolshevik. . . "

"Oh, come. Just that, sitting in this chair has finally opened my eyes a crack to some hugely painful things in this world, monumental problems I'd simply been unwilling to look at most of my. . . "

"Sitting there in that chair, you've turned your back on us, that's what you've done!" Lodge grips his arm rests, knuckles white. "Slapped me in the face!"

"Henry, for heaven's sakes. . . "

"Must be something about this room. Some—microbe the previous President left behind. May I remind you that the constitution provides for an executive branch, understood to mean that the President *executes* legislation crafted by congress. He has *not* been elected to go off on some tangent of his own and turn the country upside down."

Harding can see that further discussion is not likely to lead to anything fruitful. "All right, Henry. Let's leave it at that, shall we? Perhaps in time, you'll see what I'm getting at."

Abruptly, Lodge stands. "In time? *Time is precisely what I don't have!*"

Harding rises as well, searching his mind for a way to ease the tension. As Lodge turns sharply for the door, Harding gently palms the older man's elbow and tries giving him escort. "So," he asks, lightly, "what's Mrs. Lodge had to say about all this? Must be quite a comfort to have someone at home who entirely agrees with you—straight down the line, as I recall."

"In point of fact, Mrs. Lodge has lately shown no sympathy whatever," he snaps, pulling his arm away. "Mrs. Lodge says I'm getting exactly what I deserve —" he jerks open the door—"for having put *some colored* in the White House. Good day to—oops. . . " Lodge runs smack into Harding's black steward, knocking a tray out of his gloved hands. A porcelain tea service smashes to the floor. "Why don't you be more careful —!" Lodge snarls, and encased in his rage, flies down the hall.

Harding is taken aback by Lodge's parting volley, but the steward is positively frozen by shock, his wide eyes locked incredulously on Harding's facial features and skin tone.

Harding recovers first, kneels down, and begins picking up the pieces of crockery, laying them out on the steward's tray. "Well, Wally, it just became clear to the senator which of us was elected President. I'm afraid he took it badly." Wally remains transfixed as Harding smiles up at him. "Might you give me a hand with this? We negroes got to work together, don'tcha think?"

Late that day, Surgeon General Sawyer, a glorious vision of white and gold, paces the contrastingly olive-drab ground floor foyer of the Veterans Administration, his eye on the clock.

At 4:58 he stops pacing.

At 4:59 he nods to himself and heads for the stairs and the office of the director.

Up three flights he arrives at a glass door inscribed with "*Veterans Affairs, Charles Forbes, Director*." It swings open as Charlie's clerk, an incongruously glamorous, carefully made-up young woman, is leaving for the day. Reflexively, she gives Sawyer a slightly seductive smile as he enters and she departs, closing the door behind him.

Just inside, Sawyer encounters Charlie's secretary putting on her coat. Like the clerk, she wears an inordinate amount of make-up for daytime, and her figure could start a war. She glances with fleeting distress at the clock—5:02—but dutifully begins to remove her wrap. Sawyer smiles, shakes his head, reassures her that he can manage by himself, and sends her on her way.

She opens the door, pauses in the doorway, and murmurs, "When you're finished, General Sawyer, just press this button. The door will lock behind you."

"I will. Thank you, Miss."

"Have a good evening, sir."

Watching her through the glass door as she sashays down the hall, Sawyer wonders just where it is that Charlie recruits his office staff—and for what purposes. Then he loosens his tie, takes off his jacket, lays it on a chair, and turns to the first file cabinet.

25.

At almost that precise moment, Leland Sinclair sits on horseback, binoculars focused on the U.S. Navy's Teapot Dome installation—a collection of oil wells and elephantine storage tanks, standing in the lengthening, late-afternoon shadow of a Wyoming, teapot-shaped mountain. Two marines with rifles guard the chain-link entrance. A third has just lowered the facility's Stars and Stripes—for the last time.

When he was eighteen, Sinclair had inherited debts of $82,000, along with seven oil wells, from his wildcatter father. One of the wells actually coughed up a little petroleum now and again. The problem with the other half-dozen, Sinclair came to discover, was that even though located in the vicinity of a rich oil field, in fact within sight of several of John D. Rockefeller's highly productive rigs, his father had unimaginatively drilled them straight down. Sinclair revisited the wells, put his drillers back to work, and after burrowing about a hundred feet, altered course and headed sideways toward Rockefeller. Soon all of Sinclair's wells were every bit as productive as those of his giant competitor, who never guessed that the insignificant young upstart across the fence would have the audacity to poach Standard Oil. Thus was established a principle of oil exploration that was to make Sinclair a multi-millionaire: it is far more profitable surreptitiously sucking up other people's oil than knocking about, trying to find your own.

With his acquisition of Teapot Dome, Sinclair had achieved his apotheosis. He wouldn't have to raise one rig or drop a single hole. The navy had taken care of all that. All Sinclair need do was open the pipeline.

As the sun eases itself towards the horizon, Sinclair trains his glasses on a small military pickup truck with some dozen or so sailors in back. It rolls to the gate. The three marines toss the folded flag and their rifles to the men in the truck and scramble aboard. The truck pulls away.

Sinclair drops his binoculars back in their case, spurs his horse, and rides forward in an easy canter to inspect his new property.

26.

The following morning, in a crowded Washington courtroom a thousand miles to the east, an exceptionally melancholy Sicilian ex-bootlegger is about to learn the price of putting trust in Jess Smith.

The jury foreman rises, verdict in hand. The Sicilian, seated with his attorney at the defense table, and at the government's table, Harry Daugherty with his new protégé, boyish J. Edgar Hoover, by his side, all listen for the inevitable.

A devoté of cheap gin, Daugherty certainly harbored no animus for bootleggers. Every so often, however, the Justice Department found itself obliged to log a conviction, and the Sicilian, perhaps lulled by Jess into a false sense of security, had so blatantly thumbed his nose at the Volstead Act, Daugherty saw no choice but to finally exhibit some prosecutory zeal. "Eager J. Edgar" had taken it from there.

"We find the defendant, Marco Torrino, guilty on all four counts," intones the foreman, predictably.

The packed courtroom buzzes.

"Thank you, Mr. Foreman," says the judge without affect. "The jury is dismissed. Defendant remains free on bail till sentencing, to be held. . . " He peers over his half-glasses at his clerk as she thumbs through the calendar.

"March 18, Your Honor. 1:00 P.M. "

"March 18 at 1:00 P.M.," repeats the judge. He glares down at Marco. "I would suggest, sir, that you get your affairs in order. This court stands adjourned."

The courthouse steps are carpeted with reporters, for this trial was decidedly different. Since Prohibition, scores of bootleggers have seen their stills and bottles smashed, their trucks confiscated. Some are fined and jailed for a few weeks. The occasional egregious reoffender might be deported. But Marco bore the unhappy distinction of being the first to be headed for a federal penitentiary.

H. L. Mencken and his cub reporter are among those gathering round the embittered felon and his attorney, who fends off questions with a raised hand and a question of his own. “I ask you,gentlemen, where is there justice in putting a man in prison for delivering a sound product to a willing buyer at a fair price?”

Daugherty chooses that moment to scoot down the steps, hurrying past without so much as a sidelong glance. Marco glares at the rapidly receding figure. “Yeah,” he adds, pointedly. “While crooked politicians who don’t-a deliver, who break-a promises right and left, get away with murder.”

“What promises?” asks the cub reporter.

“What don’t they deliver?” asks another.

And then, Mencken: “Precisely *which* politicians would those be, Mr. Turino?”

Marco’s attorney whispers caution in his client’s ear. The Sicilian nods, then looks directly at Mencken. “I’ll have more to say to you about *that* when da time comes. A *lot* more.”

27.

The day for which my darling had worked so long and hard had finally arrived. From all over the world, everybody who was anybody came out to hear what he had to say about ensuring peace in this war-weary world. Can you imagine—his disarmament conference was so well-attended, the President had to personally pull strings in order to get me an invitation. Now, many years later, it's become fashionable to characterize Mr. Harding as a "do-nothing" President—an amiable, empty shell of a man who never gave serious consideration to anything. I venture to say none of his critics were there the day he opened that remarkable convention.

From every corner of the globe, diplomats and envoys have journeyed to Washington to sit beneath their nation's flags on the stage of the first Washington World Disarmament Conference. Observing the unprecedented meeting along with Nan are members of Congress and the press, contributing to an audience of 3,100, all listening with varying degrees of wonderment as the once negligible senator from Ohio turned statesman, today in black tie, initiates the proceedings in the language of a world leader.

"At this," Harding intones, "the first international disarmament conference, all of us dedicate ourselves to a world of peace, a world where the smallest people shall be secure in freedom, a world where never again will sons of one country take up weapons against sons of another. Should we succeed, then never again shall our boys—or their boys—come home crippled and maimed—or not come home at all."

Monumental applause.

But Harding has failed to captivate the entire house. Lodge and three of his isolationist colleagues, Senators Guthrie, Blair, and Paxton, sit stone-faced in the first row, arms across their chests. Seated off to one side, Wyoming's Senator Burton Wheeler finds himself wedged between two oil industry lobbyists who are working him over in stage whispers, effectively competing with Harding's speech.

"Senator," exclaims the first, "the issue isn't so much who landed Teapot Dome—it's just that Standard Oil was never given a crack at it. Mr. Rockefeller's feelings are hurt."

"No competitive bidding," moans the second. "One day it belongs to the navy. Next day old man Sinclair is in there pumping oil to beat the band."

Harding's voice resonates through the public address system. "Today we take the first concrete steps to halt the arms race!"

Senator Wheeler, a man of no small wisdom, ranks oil magnates a notch below Attila the Hun. "You're asking me to shed tears for John D. Rockefeller? Standard Oil's been shafting this country for years."

"Forever," says Harding, his voice filling the room, and bringing him another round of applause. "To the American Congress and to all nations of the world," he continues, "I shall be proposing a fair, practical, and equitable formula for dismantling some of the most terrible weapons of war."

The second lobbyist keeps his eye on the ball. "Standard Oil has *never* shafted the people of Wyoming, Senator. Montana and Utah, possibly. Never Wyoming."

"I've never given you bastards the chance," hisses Wheeler. "Why do you think I've kept Teapot Dome in navy hands all these years?"

"Today," promises Harding, "we replace the arms race—with a race for peace!"

The first lobbyist has to shout over the applause Harding brings down. "Well, the *navy* doesn't own Teapot Dome any more. *Leland Sinclair does.* My client has asked me to remind you that in the United States of America, even a ruthless son-of-a-bitch oil billionaire like John D. Rockefeller is entitled to a level playing field!"

Still applauding, much of the audience scrambles to its feet. Harding, in his glory, smiles back proudly at the standing ovation. It lasts for three minutes, perhaps the most exhilarating three minutes of Harding's political life.

With the stage lights directly in his eyes, he cannot see that Senator Lodge and his clique remain glued to their chairs, or that Senator Wheeler, profoundly troubled by what he has just learned, has summarily left the conference.

28.

H. L. Mencken, his indomitable Model-T Ford covered with 2,100 miles worth of dust, chugs up to an Albuquerque newsstand. Leaving his motor chattering, he hops out, pays his two cents for a copy of the *Albuquerque Herald*, and scans the front-page story—*"Wheeler Inquiry Into Teapot Dome Oil."* I'm missing all the fun, he muses.

He turns to the paper-seller. "Any idea how to get to the Three Rivers from here?"

The paper-seller points. "Al Fall's place? Easy. Stay on this road another, oh, quarter mile, then take the left fork. Due east. Just keep going straight. Along the creek bed. Run right into it."

"Thanks a lot. Even a city boy should be able to handle that."

The paper-seller eyes Mencken's Maryland plates. "Looks like you've been driving apiece. Didn't think there was anything that important happening in these parts."

"Maybe there isn't," replies Mencken. "Maybe there is." He climbs back into his car and shifts into gear.

Another bone-jarring twenty minutes, and Mencken pulls up to the gateway of the *"THREE RIVERS"* spread, its name branded on a new wooden sign, along with *"ALBERT FALL, PROP."* He clambers out of the car and tries the gate. Locked. He looks around, doesn't see very much, and is about to climb back behind the wheel when a fully-loaded cattle truck lumbers up, driven by an ancient cowboy. The cowboy hits the brakes, then with arthritic care slowly lowers himself out of the cab and limps to the gate. "How ya doin'?" he asks, over a cacophony of cattle sounds.

"Stayin' even," Mencken replies. "Some handsome animals you got there. Make for a hell of a barbecue."

"Don't think you'd want to do that—not at a thousand bucks a head."

"Wow! Damn expensive steak."

The cowboy nods. "These big fellas come all the way from Argentina."

"You don't say! Argentina?!"

"Prize breeders. Mr. Fall—he goes first class or he don't go." He pauses, getting just a bit suspicious. "Somethin' I can help you with?"

"Yeah—well, I heard a guy could pick up some fine land around here. Still real reasonable. Thought I'd check it out. You know—a chance to get out of the big city rat race. . . "

"Used to be."

"Used to be?"

"Used to be cheap. No more. Last six months Mr. Fall bought up damn near all of it. You lookin' for a starter spread you gotta head north. Around Alameda's your best bet."

"That far. Okay. I'll give it a look-see. Thanks for the tip." He returns to his Ford. "Seems like your boss is doing real well for himself."

The cowboy nods. "Best year in a long, long time."

"You don't say."

"Oh yeah. A while back, I didn't think the ranch was gonna make it."

Mencken shifts into gear, and tips his hat. "Amazing how fast things can turn around."

The game room in Sinclair's Georgetown mansion is dark, save for a single Tiffany lamp hanging over the billiard table. Albert Fall and Leland Sinclair play the game with considerable finesse. Sitting in the shadows next to a silver spittoon is Bobby Burns. He is content to observe; finesse has never been his strong suit.

"These are all old colleagues of mine, gentlemen," Fall insists. "Christ—*I* served on Wheeler's committee. Now Standard Oil's biting Wheeler's ass, so he's agreed to a hearing, that's all. That's what congress does when its got a problem. Hold hearings. Till the problem goes away. *This* problem will go away."

Sinclair drops the seven into a corner pocket as he addresses Burns. "Whadya think?"

"Wheeler might go easy," Burns replies, "but that old guy, Walsh—he's a fuckin' bulldog. They say once he gets hold of something, he don't let go."

"Well," Sinclair replies, "you just make sure there's nothing there for him to sink his jaws into." Burns nods, pops in a couple of aspirin and crunches down. Sinclair looks at him. "Why do you do that—chew all those damn aspirin?"

"Rotten teeth."

Sinclair shakes his head, slams the eight ball. It caroms twice and goes nowhere. "Shit," says Sinclair.

The following morning, a golf ball rolls merrily across a huge map of the world spread over the rug of the Oval Office, and drops into a cup floating on the Caribbean. Harding, enjoying a private game of miniature golf, pats himself on the back, then tees off London.

I ought to say right here that despite increasing criticism coming his way, there were still many moments when my darling truly enjoyed being President. Those first months of 1923 he took increasing satisfaction, if not in his own innate abilities—he never did give himself proper credit—then at least in what the office of the presidency could accomplish. After the big disarmament conference, he started to relax a little, taking time for himself, even sneaking off once or twice a week to play poker with Mr. Fall and some of his other old pals. And our lovemaking had become quite magical, the two of us losing ourselves in the other, traveling off to distant galaxies. It was, in fact, an especially happy period for him, I think. And for us.

But sadly, it was not to last.

There's a knock, Harding's door opens, and Mrs. Samson accompanies a solemn Dr. Sawyer into the room, his arms wrapped around a carton of files.

"Surgeon General, sir," she says, then returns to her ante room.

"Come right in, Doc, come right in. Been waiting for

you. Look at this—found a painless way to learn geography. A week ago, I couldn't tell Bermuda from Bosnia. Put that stuff down and give this putter a try." Sawyer crosses the room, gingerly negotiating Harding's global golf course. "Watch where you step," warns Harding. "Uh—careful of India there. Don't want to rile the British . . . " He sees that Sawyer is not smiling. "What is it, Doctor? Is—is it the Duchess. . . ?"

"Florence is fine, Warren. Just fine." Sawyer drops his carton on Harding's desk and starts lifting out files. "But I'm afraid you're gonna need to take a look at these, Mr. President. A good long look."

That night Harding and Sawyer, both dressed casually and incognito, slip into the Bethesda V.A. Hospital, accompanied by a solitary Secret Service man. He hangs back discreetly as Sawyer leads Harding through the wards. Harding's spirits are nearly crushed by the interminable rows of hopeless men with wrecked bodies, and by their appalling care.

The two men's journey into the Great War's dreadful aftermath ends with a visit to an astonished Zachary Cartwright. Harding embraces his old neighbor with his usual warmth, but minutes later, as he and Sawyer charge down the hospital steps towards Sawyer's Plymouth, he is, perhaps for the first time in his life, speechless with anger.

29.

Commerce Secretary Herbert Hoover waits alone in the deserted foyer to the President's Oval Office. It's well after hours, the Secret Service are off duty, and even Mrs. Samson is long gone, her desk bare, save for a jar of pencils and the desk calendar.

Hoover paces, looks at his watch, paces some more. Then, after a brief tussel with his Quaker conscience, he snoops a little, checking Samson's appointments for the day. There's his name at the bottom of the page, right after Charlie Forbes'. He shakes his head. Hoover, whose initial skepticism about Harding has turned to warm admiration, was himself known to work twenty-five hour days, eight days a week, but how many other people in government, he wonders, no less heads of state, schedule meetings from eight in the morning until ten at night?

He glances back at his watch—he's been waiting for nearly thirty minutes now. Harding has always personally ushered in his late-night visitors. Perhaps he's forgotten this last one.

Cautiously, Hoover knocks on the President's door. A moment later he hears a loud thud, followed by Harding's voice, suffused with rage: *"Those men put their lives on the line for this country, you crooked son of a bitch!"*

Reflexively, Hoover opens the door a crack, pokes his head in, and sees the President of the United States holding his Director of Veteran Affairs up by the throat, and banging him against the wall.

"How much was your kickback?" thunders Harding as he slams Charlie again. "Five cents on the dollar? A dime?" Another wallop and Charlie's glasses go flying. "You ask me for Veteran Affairs. Fine. You're my oldest friend. You want it? It's yours. This is how you thank me?!"

Wide-eyed, Hoover quickly pulls back unnoticed and silently closes the door.

Moments later it again opens and a shaken Charlie

Forbes stumbles out, clothes and hair askew; he rushes blindly past Hoover and on down the hall.

All is quiet again.

Hoover tiptoes over to Harding's open office door, listens a few seconds, then knocks on the jamb. "Mr. President?" No response. "Mr. Pres. . . "

"Herbert? Come in. Sorry you had to wait."

Hoover enters. Harding is sitting in an icy calm at his desk, hands clasped together, eyes straight ahead. "I had some—last business with Charlie."

"Er, that's fine, sir. Perhaps I should come back. . . "

"The man's a thief, Herbert. A common thief. I don't think I've ever been so hurt—so *angry* in my life." He shakes his head. "My pal. Almost forty years, if you can believe that. We used to play baseball together. Every Sunday. Back in Marion." He takes a deep breath and blows it out slowly as he turns to Hoover. "I understand you had a matter of some importance ."

"Uh yes, Mr. President. But I'm sure it can keep till . . . "

"No. It's all right." He motions to an adjacent chair. "Please —."

Hoover takes the designated seat. "I'm afraid I have more—disheartening news, sir."

"Well, better to have it all at once. No sense ruining two evenings. It's Lodge again, isn't it?"

"Yes sir." Hoover pauses. "The Senate, they're conspiring—I'm sorry, there's no other word for it—conspiring to kill your initiatives, no matter how many might benefit from them." Another pause. "There's even been a little talk of impeachment in the house. . . "

"That's absurd."

"Of course. But now with this Teapot Dome inquiry . . . "

"I'm sure Al Fall has excellent reasons for everything he did," says Harding, stiffly.

"Still, Lodge will use it against you if he can. Thinks *Congress* should be running the country. The man is vengeful. Very nearly killed Wilson."

"I know. And I helped him do it." He sighs. "Something else I have to make up for."

Harding rises, turns, and looks out the window at the Capitol Building, all aglow against the dark blue night. "The People—I'm one of them. An average American. Very average. I know it. They know it. So we talk easily, one to another. Always have. Herbert, I'm going to take my case directly to them. Yes, that's what I'm going to do." He turns back to Hoover. "To hell with the Senate. I may fall flat on my face but damn it, I'm not some two-bit political hack from Ohio. *I'm goddamn President of the United States!*"

Everything is low key and genteel in the Senate hearing room as the Harding administration's Secretary of Interior, Albert Fall, winds up his confident, righteous testimony on the second day of the Teapot Dome Inquiry. The committee investigating the matter is chaired by Fall's old friend, Burton Wheeler, assisted by a decidedly less cordial co-chairman, the venerably irascible Democrat, Francis Walsh, some congenial Republican colleagues, Dan Paxton amongst them, plus the inevitable contingent of stenographers, clerks, and assorted aides.

A navy petroleum depot in rural Wyoming is not exactly the stuff of front page news; the gallery is barely one-quarter full, and would most probably be empty were it not for H. L. Mencken's dogged curiosity, and the crying need of some impoverished, elderly citizens of Washington for a little levity in their lives, reliably provided them by Congress entirely free of charge.

Mencken and his cub reporter have planted themselves way in back, chairs tilted against the wall, taking notes, as Fall glibly pours a final dollop of oil on troubled waters. "It was my considered judgment that national security required these naval oil bases be transferred to Interior in secrecy. Teapot Dome is of small importance, gentlemen—the safety of this nation is not."

That satisfies Senator Wheeler for the moment, but owlish Senator Walsh remains suspicious. "One last question, if I may, Mr. Secretary," says Walsh.

"Of course, Senator."

"Secretary Fall, did you perchance receive any special—personal—considerations for your efforts to lease this navy oil to private parties?"

"I did *not*, sir! And I take umbrage at the suggestion!"

Apparently, so do most of the panel, who show Walsh little support. Fall, after all, is a former colleague, and a most convivial one. The vote to excuse him from further inquiry is near unanimous.

But Fall's charm cuts no ice with Mencken, who turns quietly to his cub reporter. "Hey Bud, let me give you Mencken's first law of journalism: the more vehemently a politician denies an allegation, the more likely it is to be true."

30.

Harding beams as he opens his office door for Nan, glimpsing Mrs. Samson behind her, eyebrows raised.

"Good afternoon, Mr. President," says Nurse Britton, as she makes a dignified entrance.

Harding closes the door behind her and eagerly helps her off with her coat. Today no starched white uniform: beneath the coat, Nan's hourglass form is draped in an American flag—and nothing else.

"Nan—good God!"

Nan smiles, pirouettes, unwraps herself, then using the flag as a veil, does a personal impression of Salome. Harding is delighted. "I salute your patriotism, my dear."

Nan lowers her eyes to the swelling at Harding's groin. "So I see, Mr. President." The flag slips from her hands and puddles red, white and blue at her feet.

Harding reaches for her.

With so many unpleasant matters popping up right and left and pressing on my darling's mind, each time we met I'd always make a special effort to lift his spirits. And increasingly, we'd talk about our possible future together.

Of course, back in those days, divorce for a woman was worse than death. I knew Warren could never be so cruel to Florence, for whom he would always care, however much he loved me. So I was prepared to accept our "arrangement" indefinitely, imperfect though it was. I could not imagine a life entirely without him, for I don't think I then quite saw myself a whole person. I needed Warren Harding to feel complete. And he in turn seemed unable to do without me.

Harding and Nan sprawl together in each other's arms on the sofa, under a blanket bearing the presidential seal, enjoying a post-coital glow. On the floor beside them, Nan's flag is wrapped in an embrace with Harding's trousers.

Nan kisses his cheek. "I wish. . . I wish we could be . . . a couple, Warren . . . a plain old couple—Mr. and Mrs. Anonymous."

"God, so do I, dearie. With all my heart. Just unlock my cell door and walk off. Away from this miserable place. Away from it all. Forever. With you." He sighs. "Perhaps some day."

"I can wait. I'd wait forever." She starts to kiss him again, covering his face.

"I've something to tell you, Nan."

"How much you love me."

"Well. . . yes. Beyond words. . . "

"That the sun rises and falls with my comings and goings."

"Of course, plum." Tenderly, he kisses her nose. "That—and also: I'm planning a rather long train trip. Quite an important one."

Nan sits up. "A trip? Where?"

"Across the country. You've been reading the papers, all the complimentary things my old colleague has had to say about me?"

"I try and skip over that rubbish."

Harding smiles. "But you *have* read some of it. Now and again."

"Mr. Lodge is a jealous little man. He's lost his heart. All he seems good for is tearing things down."

"Yes indeedy. Hell bent on sabotage. He intends to hog tie me in the Senate. Block each and every bill."

"Can he do that?"

"Henry? Easily. He knows all the tricks." Harding shakes his head. "And that business with Charlie Forbes. Now Al and navy oil. It all plays right into the old man's hands. So, I've decided to break out of this prison for a bit." He kisses her forehead. "I've planned a speaking tour. Almost a campaign. My idea is to travel from city to city. Much like you and I did that first time in Ohio. Look folks in the eye. Explain to them what I've been trying to do and why we ought to do it. Once The People are with me —"

"That's a *grand* idea, Warren." She bounces on his lap. "Wonderful! As soon as they hear you tell your side. . . "

"And I want you along on that train."

She stops bouncing. "You do? Really?"

"I can't possibly be away from you for almost two whole months. Two days is hard enough. . . "

"Oh Warren —! But won't Florence. . . ? I mean. . . "

"Florence and I will be traveling together, of course. You, my dear, will be tucked away somewhere in the caboose." He chuckles and kisses her on the mouth. "Mixed in with a bunch of White House aides. Now it won't be easy but I'm sure there'll be ways we can. . . "

She wraps herself around him. "Oh, Mr. President!" A kiss, long and deep, as they stretch out together. Nan, ecstatic and energetic, maneuvers herself atop him, rubbing her lush body up and down his.

"Wow. . . Nan. . . Sweet Nan. . . Nan. . . " In moments he enters her.

She thrusts against him. "Oh yes, my dear, yes—oh please, Warren, please. . . "

Harding rises to the challenge as the two experienced lovers quickly drive the other towards climax. Nan feels life itself within her.

And then—Harding gasps. "Whew, Nan, wait. . . "

"Oh Warren, I can't. . . "

"Dearie, wait—gotta catch my breath. . . "

"Warren —? Warren, what's the matter?"

"Whew. Let me. . . sit up." He does, pressing his fist to the center of his chest. "Have this pressure—right here. Whew." He can barely breathe.

Nan is frightened. "Are you going to be alright?"

"Sure. . . just. . . a little winded. Jeez, Nan, I'm five times. . . your age. Gotta. . . go a bit easy, sweet."

Florence Harding, crocheting by the bay window in her White House quarters, puts down her work as the Harding's personal butler, Dirkson, a dignified and distinguished-looking, elderly black man arrives with the day's newspapers. She scans the front pages with dismay.

> *"V.A. HOSPITALS—QUESTIONS RAISED"*
> *"WASHINGTON MYSTERY—WHERE'S CHARLIE?"*
> *"MORE TEAPOT DOME ALLEGATIONS"*

"Has the president seen these, Dirkson?"

"No ma'am. He's still having his treatment. I left copies with Mrs. Samson. . . "

"Treatment? What treatment?"

"I'm sorry, I don't know, ma'am. I just know a nurse attends him every week or so."

She looks at him open-jawed. "A nurse —." This is the first she's heard of any nurse. "All right. Thank you, Dirkson."

As Dirkson silently withdraws, Florence stares at her crocheting, lying on the sill. Then, brow furrowed, she rises, goes to the telephone and dials four digits.

Downstairs in the Oval Office, Harding is starting to feel somewhat better. The intercom on his desk buzzes twice—Harding picks up the earpiece, and what he hears knocks the wind out of him once again.

"Thank you, Betsy." Hurriedly he replaces the earpiece, his breathing labored. "Nan, Florence is—on her way down."

"What? Here?" She leaps for her coat.

Harding starts scrambling back into his clothes. "She's never. . . done this. . . before," he wheezes.

"Warren, dear God. . . "

"I'm. . . fine, Nan. Just. . . button up," he gulps a breath, "and let's try and get you out of here."

Florence, her jaw set, leaves the private living quarters and chugs down the corridor as fast as her cane will go.

One floor beneath, Harding quickly rolls up and hands Nan the flag, then her shoes, and starts maneuvering her, still barefoot and pinning her hair together, towards the door. "No, wait. Not that way. Come. Over here."

Florence has made it down the elevator to the ground floor now, her cane biting into a plush hall runner as she takes a sharp turn for the Oval Office.

Inside, Harding is pulling the drawstring on a curtain that conceals a narrow side door. "One of the. . . Secret Service boys will. . . get you out." He struggles to breathe. "Christ, I'm—so sorry Nan. . . "

He unlocks and guides her into the slim passageway. She can scarcely bear to leave him.

"Warren, I'm very, very worried. . . "

"I'll be fine, dearie." He manages a winded kiss. "Please. . . "

Nan forces herself down the little corridor. Harding re-draws the curtain, then hastily finishes dressing, all the while breathing shallowly, perspiration on his brow. He's just buttoning up his fly when there's a familiar knock. He cinches his belt and dabs his forehead with his handkerchief.

A louder knock. Harding puts the best possible face on his intense physical discomfort—and guilt. "Come on in!" The door opens and Mrs. Samson and Florence appear. Florence enters, Samson withdraws. "Florence, whatever are you. . . ?"

"I'm sorry if I interrupted anything, Wurr'n. But I—I was concerned. Dirkson just told me you've been receiving some sort of treatments. . . "

"Treatments? What —? Uh. . . oh, that. It's nothing, Duchess." He forces out a small laugh. "Vitamin injections, that's all. Doc Sawyer—prescribed them. You know how tired I was for a while." He flops down heavily on the sofa, trying, with little success, to conceal his breathlessness. "Come, sit by me."

She looks at him with alarm, then slowly settles down next to him. "Wurr'n you don't— look that well. You've just *had* a treatment?" He nods and works on his breathing. She is finding it painful to watch. "I think we should call Doc Sawyer. . . "

"Really, Duchess. Just need to sit. For a moment." "
She studies him closely. "The . . . er, nurse . . . is she . . . ?"
"She had other—calls." He manages a deep breath, even a wan smile. "Please. Don't worry. Going to be fine . . . "
The intercom buzzes. Harding hauls himself back up, steps to his desk and flips the device on. Mrs. Samson is at the other end.
"Ask him to wait," says Harding, into the receiver. "Just a few more minutes."
He clicks off and turns to Florence. "Duchess, Herbert Hoover is here. He's helping with my new speeches. Going to need a lot of them." Harding is able to take a solid breath now; he exhales slowly. "Good ones."
"Wurr'n, if there's something wrong, please, you must . . ."
"There's plenty wrong, my dear—it's called the United States Senate."
"All right." Reluctantly, she rises. "Promise you'll make it an early evening?"
"If I possibly can." He embraces her, then guides her to the door.
Hoover is waiting in the foyer. Accustomed to Nurse Britton emerging at about this time, he blinks twice when Florence comes out instead, Harding just behind her. "Mrs. Harding —!"
"Good afternoon, Mr. Secretary. A pleasure to see you again."
"Thank you, ma'am. It's always. . . "
"Mr. Secretary, Wurrn's been feeling a bit peaked. I trust you won't keep him a moment longer than absolutely necessary."
"Ma'am, just yesterday Mrs. Hoover gave *me* an ultimatum—either the President of the United States, or her. I assured her: no contest."
Florence nods, partially appeased. Harding, his breathing easier, reaches for her hand and squeezes it tenderly.

31.

It is long past midnight, and the Lincoln Memorial is deserted, save for Jess Smith, Harry Daugherty, and the great marble figure of Abraham Lincoln, seated on his throne, surveying the Capitol Mall.

Jess hands Daugherty a fat, currency-sized envelope. "That reporter—Mencken," says Jess. "Keeps nosing around. Been trying to locate Charlie."

Daugherty slips the envelope into a breast pocket. "Will he find him?"

Jess shakes his head. "Charlie sails in two hours. Calais."

"Calais should be lovely this time of year. How's Charlie holding up?"

"Actually, he's not. He"s saying that when he comes back, we're supposed to 'protect' him."

"Don't think we can do that." He looks at Jess meaningfully. "Everyone's got to stand on his own feet. This little Mencken problem—has Burns come up with anything yet?"

"Oh, sure. The guy's a teetotaler. Drives a twelve-year-old Ford. Has an ex-wife in Baltimore. . . "

Daugherty brightens. "Ex-wife?"

"— Who's still in love. And according to Burns, Mencken pays his alimony and child support like clockwork. In advance. The guy's a goddamn saint."

"Yeah, well, Burns will find something—even if he has to invent it." He makes a fist and feints a tap to Jess'chin. "You know, Jess, you don't always arrange things with me before making promises. Some mighty big promises."

"I—I didn't want to be bothering you all the time. . . "

"You're never a bother, Jess. You oughta know that by now." He embraces him, then stands back and fixes him in his gaze. "Please—always check with me first. You don't want to find yourself stuck out there all by yourself. Dangerous place."

Jess nods. Daugherty smiles, reaches out, and tussles Jess' hair.

Lincoln looks down at the loving conspirators with a heavy heart.

PART SIX

32.

Whenever preparing for a trip, however brief, Nan's usual remedy for her intractable difficulty sorting out clothing she might actually use from that better left behind was simply to take along almost everything she owned. Today, however, the suitcase open on her bed and a giant steamer trunk on the floor are both nearly full, and she has yet to address the overriding question of evening wear.

Nan glances at her night-table clock—barely an hour to complete her packing. She hurries to her walk-in closet and fingers three dresses. Should she take the red, the green, or the beige? She holds the red one against her and looks down at her waistline—seems to have gained a little weight. Best to be safe—bring all three.

She lifts the hangers off the bar and is just carrying them over to the bed when her doorbell rings. She drapes the dresses over the headboard, goes to the front door and checks through the peephole. Then, very nearly dumb-struck, she slowly opens up to the Secretary of Commerce.

"Good morning, Miss Britton," says Herbert Hoover. "Forgive me for intruding on you like this. But we have—a problem."

"A—a problem?"

"I was hoping you'd be able to help."

Nan remains rooted to the ground.

"Might I come in?"

"Oh—of course, Mr. Hoover." She recovers a portion of her wits and leads him into the living room. "Please—won't you sit down. Er, may I offer you anything?"

"I'm fine. Thank you." He settles uneasily into her easy chair. "Pleasantly cool for July, wouldn't you say?"

"Yes, sir. I was thinking the very same thing. Just this morning."

Hoover takes a long moment to gather his thoughts. "This is difficult for me, Miss Britton. . . "

Nan turns pale and drops down on the edge of an adjacent chair. "Warren —! Has something happened to. . . ?"

"The President's feeling very well. Quite eager about this big trip of his. 'Raring to go," he told me."

Nan is relieved—somewhat.

"Miss Britton—Nan—may I call you Nan?" "

She nods—cautiously.

"I've come to speak with you in confidence, Nan. Entirely on my own initiative. But I believe—I'm quite certain—our interests coincide." Delicately, Hoover ventures into the mine field. "The President's speaking tour—it's of supreme importance—for him, for the nation, for everything he's tried to do these past two and a half years. I think he will succeed—you know how he is, once you get him in front of a crowd." She does, and can't help but smile. "And you know, as do I," Hoover continues, "that Warren Harding is a man of simple, great integrity. But. . . "

He massages his knuckles earnestly as he struggles to find the words. There were probably any number of ways to say what he knew had to be said, none of them good. "There have been those around the President who. . . " He pauses, then starts again. "There's the stench of scandal in Washington, Nan, terrible scandal, and it's drifting toward the White House. In time, it's almost certain to raise questions, even questions about the President himself. Be assured, the press will be crawling all over that train, every one of them looking for. . . God knows what." Tactfully, he looks away. "I've long known how—close you are to the President. Others must at least suspect."

Nan bites her lip—sensing what's coming.

Hoover turns back to her. "Many men, even heroic men, can be blinded by their desires. By their enormous capacity for love." He pauses. "These next seven weeks may well be the most crucial in the Harding presidency. Nan, *you* must decide."

Tears come to her eyes as she shakes her head. Gently, Hoover persists. "I believe Warren Harding can be recorded by history as a great President. Or he can continue to be with you. But not both."

33.

So accustomed has Mencken become to the buzz and jangle of the *Baltimore Sun* newsroom that a quiet setting can cut his writing speed in half. But here at his war-scarred desk, he's in his element. His two-finger attack gracelessly efficient, he types the last of his final pages of the day in record time, jerks it out of the Underwood and crumples the carbon paper, dropping it with the others into the trash. Finished with minutes to spare.

Mencken slides the four-page original into a large manila envelope and scratches on an address. He hesitates for a second, then tosses it on top of his "Out-go" basket, adjacent to a scrawny avocado tree living, none too happily, in a twelve inch clay pot.

Sweeping up the newsroom, the newest janitor to be hired by the *Sun* watches out of the corner of his eye as the paper's most celebrated journalist stands and looks over at his protégé, banging away at the desk opposite his. "”Well, Bud," says Mencken, "off to cover my worst nightmare—three flatulent Harding speeches a day. For seven weeks!"

"I thought lately he was starting to sound pretty good," replies the cub, continuing to type.

Mencken locks the four-page onionskin copy in his desk drawer and covers his typewriter. "He always *sounds* fine. What he needs to do is track down a few coherent ideas to go with those gaseous high-flying phrases. He's always had the words, now if he can only find his voice. . . "

"I take it you don't think our President has all that much upstairs."

"Strictly single-story. Remember, this is the guy who appointed the hometown mailman postmaster general, and put his wife's G.P. in charge of public health. Not that Harding's dumb, particularly. Just that blood intended to supply his brain may have been diverted down to another organ. Hey, water my tree, will you, Bud?"

"You really think you'll get avocados off that thing?"

"Some day." Mencken pats the manila envelope. "If

you're patient, all manner of things bear fruit. Meanwhile I'll bring a couple back for you from California."

"Yuck. Bring back Clara Bow. I think she'd enjoy touring Washington. With me."

"Clara Bow, huh?"

The cub stops typing and grins wickedly. "I like 'em young and loose."

"Rumor has it, you're not the only one. You might have to fight off our President."

"Nah," says the cub. "They say he already has his own. Home-grown."

Mencken laughs, winks, and is on his way.

The janitor swings over, his eye on the envelope Mencken's left behind. But he's a few seconds slow. The messenger-boy rushes by, scoops up Mencken's outgoing mail, dumps it into a big sack with all the others—and hurries off. The janitor grimaces in frustration—then studies the wastepaper basket. He glances up furtively—everyone's focused elsewhere. Quickly, the janitor stoops down and extracts Mencken's crumpled carbons.

A full-dress motorcycle escort, lights on and sirens wailing, leads Harding and his entourage to the President's train, *The Superb*, awaiting them under a blanket of flags at platform eleven of Washington's Union Station. Technicians are already there, lugging the latest in amplifying equipment, along with radio relay cables and cases of vacuum tubes. Several minutes later, Harding, Florence, Sawyer, Hoover, Samson, and a coterie of Secret Service start to board the train, all blinking at a blizzard of flashbulbs.

Harding pauses at the top step, turns, waves for the reporters and photographers crowding round, and at the same time manages to look up and down the length of the platform, hoping for a glimpse of Nan. No luck.

And then, wait, *yes*, isn't that her, heading for the next-to-last car?

For a moment the young woman in his line of sight

turns her face towards him as she climbs into the train—no, he was mistaken.

Nan is in fact standing at her living room window, looking off unseeing towards the Jefferson Memorial, eyes red, her tears all but exhausted.

I had wanted desperately to be on that train. I had so wanted to shout at Mr. Hoover, ***no****, I cannot do what you ask—I love Warren Harding for the man he is here in the present moment, not the President of some far off biography. No, Mr. Hoover. I need to be with him. Now and forever.*

But at the last minute, my selfishness met its limits. I loved him more than I loved myself.

The President's pullman, a rolling palace of rose-wood, brass, velvet, and beveled glass, is beginning to slide out of the station when Mrs. Samson appears with a sheaf of papers. "These just caught up with us, Mr. President."

"Thank you, Betsy," says Harding as he takes them from her. He shuffles through them with minimal interest until he comes to a letter addressed to him in a familiar female hand, green ink, and marked *"PERSONAL."*" He carries it into his sleeping compartment, sits down on the bed, tears it open and begins to read. His face drops.

Harding is but one of several to receive dispiriting news that day.

In his Senate office, Senator Walsh hands his aide a four-page document. "I'll need a synopsis for the committee, Carl. Keep it under a page, please, and maybe, just maybe, it'll get read."

"Yes, Senator."

"Oh—and best lock up the original. I believe it constitutes legal evidence."

"Yes, sir. I'll have everything done by tonight."

Walsh nods and heads out the door. "I know you will, Carl, I know you will."

Carl takes his assignment into his office, closes the door and scans the document. Then he picks up the phone and dials the private line of the Director of the FBI.

Bobbie Burns, a cigarette jammed in his mouth, answers the phone on its first ring. The caller gets right to the point. Burns recognizes Carl's voice.

"Not looking good, Mr. Burns. Let me read something to you."

Albert Fall and a ripe young woman in buckskin, side by side on horseback, gallop up to the Three Rivers ranch-house. The old cowboy comes out on the porch to greet them, a telegram in hand, giving it to Fall as he takes the reins of the woman's horse.

"Came about an hour ago, boss."

Fall rips it open, his face grim. His riding companion dismounts, saunters over, and leans against his thigh, trying for a little extra attention. Fall finishes the telegram, wads it up into a ball, then looks down at his friend and squeezes out an unconvincing smile.

34.

Though not physically present, I was very much with Mr. Harding in spirit as his train traveled across the land. It was an unprecedented trip. I do not believe any President had ever before gone out and personally met so many of his countrymen. Mr. Harding journeyed to their towns and cities, large and small, to their streets and parks, to their Rotaries, to their county fairs. He shook tens of thousands of hands, and reached many thousands more citizens through the miracle of radio. In the week since his departure I had already accumulated two scrapbooks of news clippings—wonderful photos of my darling addressing the multitude from dozens of different podiums, at train depots, grange halls, sports stadiums, school auditoriums, civic squares, even fire stations. And no matter when or where he spoke, people would reach out to touch him. They understood that though he was President of the United States, he remained just one of them. I must confess, during this time I took to harboring one of his handkerchiefs. On a lark I had snuck one out of his breast pocket shortly before he left, and the linen was still rich with his scent. Now I would listen to his reassuring voice on the airwaves while holding this cherished piece of cloth to my face, and pretend he was there in my living room, talking just to me.

Harding, standing on *The Superb's* rear platform with Florence by his side, winds up an address to a small, lukewarm audience at the Wheeling train station.

"People of West Virginia, help me to remind the Senate—this tiny group of willful old men—that this country still belongs to you. Thank you and God bless."

A few scattered cheers, some polite applause, but Harding senses that he's not connecting. Nevertheless he and Florence wave, then retreat back into the train, as technicians swarm out and begin pulling wires.

Harding and Florence make their way to the President's

pullman, where Hoover, Sawyer, Samson, and the butler, Dirkson, await. Harding turns to Hoover. "You and I will be burning the midnight oil again, Herbert. That last speech just didn't have it."

"You're still warming up today, Mr. President," says Hoover.

"Yeah. I need warming up. Dirkson, let me have a small one. How about the rest of you?" They all shake their heads. "God," Harding continues, "what a relief to be away from Washington and the Anti-Saloon League's prying eyes. Quite sure you won't have a snort, Herbert?"

"Quite sure, Mr. President."

"Goddamn busybodies. Shades of the Inquisition. How 'bout it, Doc? This is pre-war hooch."

"Maybe later, Warren."

Harding turns to Mrs. Samson. "Mm. Dispatches arrive yet, Betsy?"

"While you were speaking, sir." She hands him a packet.

He thumbs through it. "What in blazes —? Al testified two entire days last month." He turns to Hoover. "*Now* what the hell does the Senate want of him?"

"Apparently there have been some—new developments," replies Hoover, diplomatically.

Harding sits down heavily and starts to read of his Secretary of Interior's latest misfortunes. His breathing seems labored. Each document appears more distressing than the last. "Jesus Christ!" He passes them on to Hoover. "And Dirkson, let's make that a double."

Sawyer and Florence exchange concerned looks.

The following morning finds Albert Fall again in the Senate Committee hearing room fielding questions, this time less confident and less righteous. He's also brought along a lawyer. The chairman of the committee, Burton Wheeler, is not there today to guide the inquiry; unfortunately for Fall, Francis Walsh is in his place.

Nan watches morosely from the gallery. Herbert Hoover's admonitions about a dark cloud of scandal rolling inexorably towards the White House have stayed with her, intensifying profoundly her sense of herself as presidential protector and champion.

The Senate hearings are far better attended now than were the opening sessions a few weeks ago, and the atmosphere notably less cordial— Senator Walsh poses questions like the federal prosecutor he once was. "Secretary Fall, would you be so kind as to explain to this committee why you pushed to have all the national parks transferred to your department?"

"Far more cost-effective with them consolidated under one bureau, Senator Walsh. The less government, the better. Efficiency and streamlining—that's the way government should be going."

Walsh gives Fall his most owlish squint. "Some of us were just a little concerned the national parks might be going the way of the navy's oil. Or perhaps the Veterans Hospitals."

Nan can't help but overhear the wisecracks of two Washington wags seated just behind her.

"Surprised these guys haven't sold off the White House furniture," says one.

"With the President still in the bed," sniggers the other.

Nan whirls around in her seat. "Oh why don't the two of you *shut up!*"

Senator Walsh puts on his reading glasses, a sure sign that he's getting to the more nettlesome details, and thumbs through four well-underlined sheets of paper. Then he looks down at Fall, fixing him with a cold stare, like a biologist pinning an insect.

"Mr. Secretary, it has come to our attention that your ranch in New Mexico recently tripled in size. Just about the time those oil leases went to Sinclair. Coincidental, you think?"

Fall confers with his attorney, sitting alongside, then grapples with the question. He'd sooner juggle hot coals.

"As previously testified, Senator, all my official endeavors, including decisions regarding Teapot Dome, have always been entirely independent of my personal financial interests. I should add, sir, that those oil reserves were all transferred to Mr. Sinclair with the *President's* approval. His *written* approval."

The press, as if of one mind, begins to scribble furiously.

"Yes," sighs Walsh, sadly, almost to himself. "I'm keenly aware of that, Mr. Secretary. Keenly aware."

Late that afternoon, Leland Sinclair gets his turn at the witness table. It does not go well. He's barely testified ten minutes, when Walsh, seething with exasperation, interrupts. "I put it to you again, sir—have you ever been party to *any* personal financial transactions with Secretary Fall?"

"I am a private citizen, Senator. I don't see where my financial affairs are any of this committee's business." He pauses. "But, I believe I did make him— a small loan. You understand, Al Fall and I go back a long ways. . . "

"A small loan—how small a loan, Mr. Sinclair?"

"Seems to me it was on the order of. . . two hundred fifty thousand dollars."

Nan winces as a shock-wave ripples through the room. It reaches Walsh. *"Two hundred fifty thousand dollars?"* he asks.

"Petty cash, Senator. A man with my net worth. . . "

"I'm sure, Mr. Sinclair. And you made a loan of this 'petty cash' in expectation of what?"

"In expectation of what?"

"Secretary Fall gets the money. What, sir, did you expect of *him*?"

"I expected that he'd pay the goddamn money back."

There's a bit of relieved laughter from the spectators. But Walsh isn't laughing. "I see. And has he paid it back?"

Sinclair thinks for several long moments and then replies, "I don't believe he has. No, sir. Not as yet."

Reporters start to crowd noisily towards the door.

"Thank you, Mr. Sinclair," says Walsh. "You're

excused. For now." He turns to his colleagues. "Time for our evening recess, gentlemen?"

The room reverberates with ever louder chatter and the sound of chairs scraping, as most in attendance start filing out. But Sinclair isn't done. "I want to add, Senator: Secretary Fall is a great public servant. If ever he left government service, I'd be honored to take him into my employ."

Walsh replies over the sharply increasing din. "Seems to me, Mr. Sinclair, you've already done precisely that."

The room gradually empties, save for Nan. She remains in her seat, immobilized by despair.

35.

Needless to say, Mr. Sinclair's testimony didn't exactly help matters. It was in the papers for days. Even more distressing was Mr. Fall's shameless suggestion that my Warren was somehow mixed up in all this monkey business. I was so mad, I do believe I could have strangled the man. But vexing though all this was, I now had to turn my attention to a personal problem of my very own.

Nan push-pulls a carpet sweeper across her living room rug with religious zeal. Suddenly she's hit with a wave of nausea. She swallows hard, sits down, and waits for the feeling to pass.

It doesn't.

She rises and hurries to the bathroom, gags, but doesn't quite upchuck. She takes a deep breath, then a glass of water. Feels better.

Just as she's heading out of the bathroom, she catches her profile in the full-length mirror fastened to the towel cabinet door. She stops, looks down at her breasts, then back again at their image in the mirror. Placing her hands under her bosom, she lifts up gently.

Medical confirmation of Nan's pregnancy is seismic in its impact. Finishing up with the obstetrician's nurse, Nan still wears a dazed smile.

"Then," says the nurse, "during your last trimester, doctor will probably want to check weekly." She places a card bearing next month's appointment in Nan's hand. Nan stares at it. "Any guesses, Mrs. English?" asks the nurse.

"Guesses?"

"Boy or girl?"

"Yes. Boy or girl."

"What?"

"I mean, I'm sure my husband would be equally delighted. With either."

36.

By mid-July Harding has pressed the flesh in nearly half the forty-eight states, delivered some three dozen speeches explaining his programs and roasting his Senate opposition, given impetus to an epidemic of German measles by kissing several hundred babies, and publicly consumed an entire poultry farm's worth of chicken dinners.

Today, making a last stop in Indiana before beginning the western leg of his trip, he is taken on a tour of a state-of-the-art steel mill by its owner, industrialist Jordan Gary. Steel workers stop and gape as Harding shakes every hand within reach. Gary, straining to hold Harding's attention, points to freshly milled sheets of steel, stacked twenty feet high. "Our new stainless process, Mr. President. Never rusts."

"Is that right."

"Once we mill a sheet of Gary steel, it's part of this planet forever."

Two coalers amble by and are startled to find themselves vigorously shaking hands with the President of the United States. "Hello, how are you? I'm Warren Harding. Good to see you." Harding seems untroubled that his right hand is now black with coal dust.

Gary pursues his agenda. "But as you see, sir, it's all very labor intensive. You go ahead with this legislation of yours to eliminate the twelve-hour day, my industry would have to hire on another sixty thousand men."

"Glad to hear it, Mr. Gary. I've always stood for full employment." He extends his hand to another worker. "How do you do, sir."

"Mr. President," Gary persists, "I must tell you we were a little disappointed. After supporting your ticket with nearly a half-million dollars. . . "

"Well if you boys have that kind of cash to spread around, you ought to be able to afford a few more workers, don't you think?"

He smiles at Gary as they turn a corner to face another

string of workers, several not more than fourteen years of age. Harding reaches for the hand of one of the youngest. "Good afternoon to you, laddie. I'm Warren Harding. Shouldn't you be in school?"

That night, a far less ebullient Harding tramps up and down the length of the presidential pullman as *The Superb* speeds west through the darkness. Hoover, Sawyer, Florence, and White House counsel Travis remain seated around him, resonating with his concern. Newspapers, their front pages all trumpeting the Teapot Dome story, are scattered everywhere.

Harding turns to Travis. "If Al Fall says it was a loan, it was a *goddamn loan.*"

Travis shakes his head. "So far, Sinclair's not been able to 'find' the promissory note. And even if it actually was a loan—which we seriously doubt—the timing. . . "

"I've worked with Al since I came to Washington. He's a close personal friend. Played poker with the man a hundred times. He *doesn't* cheat."

Sawyer pipes up. "Not for a ten dollar pot."

"Perhaps," says Travis, "if the President would consider. . . "

"I don't want to hear any more!" Harding shouts, then immediately regrets his loss of temper. "Sorry, Mr. Travis. Didn't mean to snap. Just worn out. What say we all have a pick-me-up? Then Herbert, you and I can go to work on my address for tomorrow. . . "

"Go to work?" asks Sawyer. "Warren, you gave your word. Now before you do anything else, spare me fifteen minutes."

"Doc, I'm *fine*. All I need is one good night's sleep. Bouncing all night on this train—I swear it must have square wheels. . . "

"Please, Wurr'n," begs Florence. "Your breathing seemed so labored last night. Why not let Doc check you over. Just to be sure."

Harding gives a little snort. "C'mon people, do I look ill?"

They look at him in silence.

Harding acquiesces with a sigh. "All right, Doctor. That's what we pay you for, isn't it."

Harding sits on the bed of his sleeping compartment, shirt off, as Sawyer listens to his heart and lungs with a stethoscope. "How the hell can you hear anything over this train?" Harding asks.

"I can hear fine if you'd just keep your mouth shut. Okay, take a deep breath. Let it out slow." Harding complies. "Again."

Sawyer lifts the stethoscope from his ears. "Thank you, Mr. President. You can put your shirt back on again."

"Still ticking?"

"Barely. Might be a bit of fluid in your right lung. Just a little. Can't be sure. We'll go over it again tomorrow. I still think you could drop some of the smaller cities. . . "

"*No*. I'll be all right." He starts to rise.

"Uh, don't get up just yet, Warren. Some news a man takes better sittin' down."

Harding shoots him a puzzled look but obediently settles back on the edge of the bed as Sawyer continues. "I spoke to Nan."

Harding jumps up again. "You son of a gun. You did? When? How. . . ?"

"She managed to get a call through to me. Back in Indiana."

"God, I wish I could have heard her voice. Why didn't you—? Christ, I miss her. Maybe at the next stop we could figure a way—what did she say? Is she. . . ?"

"She asked me to tell you"—he pulls a slip of paper from his vest pocket and reads—"'that all her thoughts are with you. Morning, noon and night.'" He clears his throat. "Especially at night." Harding looks down at his feet. "And that she's pregnant," continues Sawyer. "Three, maybe four months."

"What?!" The train jerks and bounces over a rough patch of track. Harding slowly sinks back on the bed. "Mother of God. Why didn't she say any. . . ?"

"It's *her* first time too, Warren. She missed—or ignored all the signs."

For the greater part of a minute, Harding just sits, fist to his chin, sifting through the feelings flooding through him. "The poor little dear." He looks at Sawyer. "How is she—? Does she sound . . . ?"

"Now that she's gotten past the initial shock, I believe she's quite pleased. Actually she was worried about how *you* would take the news. But *she's* happy, I think."

"She wants the baby."

"Oh yes. She wants the baby."

"Good. That's good."

Sawyer observes him closely. "Sure you're okay?"

Harding nods. "We'll certainly have some sorting out to do when we get back to Washington, won't we." He rises from the bed, a half-smile gliding across his face. He catches his image in the window glass. "Doc, aren't I old to be having a child?"

"If I remember my biology, Warren, it's the age of the mother that seems to make a difference."

37.

Jess Smith's new Washington home is a model of what bad taste can achieve when money is no object—a top-of-the-line mélange of garish colors and mismatched styles. Jess, in bathrobe and slippers, emerges from the kitchen carrying a gold-plated tray with his breakfast—a mound of jelly donuts, cup of coffee, shot glass of whiskey, pack of cigarettes—the four basic food groups; plus the morning paper. He places the tray on a stand that arches over a velvet purple chaise longue, swats his cat off the cushion, settles in, and begins to eat and read. The *Washington Post's* front page is almost entirely taken up by Harding's *"PROPOSALS FOR A BETTER WORLD,"* and a large artist's sketch of Harding delivering a speech. Teapot Dome is relegated to a small corner box. Jess nods cynically.

The doorbell rings. He ignores it and fires up a cigarette. The bell rings repeatedly. Then stops. Jess sips his coffee and reads.

The telephone rings. It rings again and keeps on ringing. Jess sighs, stuffs in a last chunk of donut, pushes the breakfast tray aside, rises, pads across the room to the telephone table and picks up the phone.

"Jess Smith," he says, mouth full.

His face falls. "What? They wouldn't dare." He listens. "I don't give a rat's ass. . . "

The doorbell starts ringing again and won't quit.

"Hold on a second." He drops the phone, charges over to the front door, opens it, and finds a uniformed delivery man bearing a bouquet of flowers.

"Smith? Mr. Jess Smith?" asks the delivery man, pleasantly.

"Who wants to know?"

"I got this delivery."

"Yeah okay, I'm Mr. Jess Smith and I'm on the goddamn phone."

Puzzled and annoyed, he grabs for the flowers, while simultaneously the delivery man reaches into the bouquet, draws out a folded document, slaps it into Jess' outstretched right hand, then shoves the flowers in his left.

"Federal subpoena, Mr. Smith. Er, you oughta put those in water."

Two businessmen conferring with Harry Daugherty in the Justice Department's auxiliary conference room have just taken out their checkbooks when there's a knock on the door. It opens part way and Daugherty's secretary sticks her head in. "Sorry to disturb you, sir, but it's Mr. Smith again. It's the third time he's called."

"Ah. Tell him I'm in a meeting, Matilda. Tell him—tell him I expect to be tied up all day."

She nods and withdraws. Daugherty turns back to his visitors. "Just never enough hours in the day."

Both businessmen sign, tear out their checks, and hand them over to Daugherty. "We're appreciative you were able to squeeze us in," says one.

"Most appreciative," says the other.

"The Attorney General is a public servant, gentlemen. Please, feel free to come to me any time."

Another dedicated public servant, FBI Director Bobby Burns, flips the "respond" switch of his office intercom as he nods goodbye to the janitor from the *Baltimore Sun*, just heading out the door, then growls into his microphone. "Yeah, I'll see him." He switches off, eats two aspirin, then stands and looks out the window at the Bureau's parking lot three stories below.

Jess flies in, clutching his subpoena. "What the hell's *this*?"

Burns remains at the window, watching unhappily as a small dog relieves itself on the fender of his Stutz. "You're in good company," he says. "I got one this morning. So did Roxie Forbes—Charlie's wife? A few other people. Mind closing the door?"

Jess slams the door. “What other people?”

Burns turns to face him. “Harry, for one. The Committee’s had the gall to subpoena the Attorney General of the United States.”

“They subpoenaed Harry? Can they do that?”

“They just did. Have a seat, Jess.” Burns returns to his desk and begins clipping his nails.

“I don’t feel like sitting,” says Jess. “You’re mighty calm.” He sits anyway. “You knew those subpoenas were coming.”

Burns nods. “Its my business to know.”

“All right, what the hell am I supposed to do. . . ?”

“Now don’t get your knickers in a bunch. I’ll handle things.”

“Yeah? You gonna handle my appearance before the Senate?”

“Just tell the distinguished members of the committee that you don’t know.”

“Don’t know what?”

“Whatever the hell they ask. You got no idea what they’re talking about. If they start getting too nosey, take the Fifth. Why do you think this great nation has a god-damn Constitution?” He pops a couple more aspirin into his mouth and bites down. “It was practically written for you, Jess.”

38.

Jess gets his audience before the Wheeler Committee on Tuesday, August 3rd. He could have mailed in his testimony. "I decline to answer on grounds that it may tend to incriminate me," he says for the twelfth consecutive time.

Senator Walsh presses him. "Mr. Turino further testified that shortly before his bootlegging conviction he gave you large cash payments in return for promises of immunity? Is that true?"

"I decline to answer on grounds that it may tend to incriminate me."

Walsh shakes his head in disgust and passes the microphone back to Chairman Wheeler. "Mr. Smith," asks Wheeler, "please tell this committee what you know about the German munitions manufactory, Brockmann and Schmidt."

"I—I decline to answer on grounds. . . "

Wheeler cuts him off. "Sir, do you realize you've yet to respond to a single one of our questions?"

"Guess you can't please all of the people all of the time," Jess replies, feebly. "Abraham Lincoln said that, I think."

The Senators look at each other. Walsh motions to Wheeler for the microphone's return, then tries a different tack. "Mr. Smith—have you ever had an arrangement, *any* sort of arrangement, with the Attorney General?"

Jess blanches. "I—I decline to answer. . . "

"You and Harry Daugherty were quite close, weren't you? *Personally*, I mean."

There's a long pause. Then Jess answers in a soft voice. "Yes. We were."

"And the President—you've been on a first name basis since his Ohio days, isn't that so? Quite a long time." No response from Jess. Walsh pressures him. "Mr. Smith?" A murmur bubbles up and begins rippling through the room.

"Yes, sir," replies Jess, finally, his usual high tenor pushing up into the castrato range. "Quite a long time."

Languidly, Nan tilts back and forth in her living room rocker, surrounded by books on childrearing, but reading one entitled *"Preparatory Schools of America."*

It was getting harder for me to keep focused on the shenanigans in Washington. I found myself thinking all the time about our baby to-be. And of course, the child's dear father. I lived for the day of his return. Meanwhile, I cherished his letters. How beautifully he expressed himself.

Several envelopes slither through the mail slot of Nan's front door. She jumps up, collects, thumbs through the letters, finds and tears open the one she's been waiting for.

Harding, seated at the little desk of his sleeping compartment, defies the train's motion as he again puts his feelings for Nan down on paper in what has become their daily correspondence.

You have given me a future, dearest. How very different my world would have been had you not ventured into it. How much of life I would have missed. But not a day passes, dear one, that I don't think of all the pleasures of youth you've sacrificed just to be with me now and again. I will not have you weighed down with worry, as well. I've made certain arrangements . . .

He glances out the window, sees that they're pulling into a station jammed with people, then resumes writing.

You will want for nothing, my love. That, I promise. You and the child. Yes, Nan, I know, I too wish we could simply be. . .

A knock on the door.

"Yes?"

"Denver, Mr. President," replies Dirkson through the door. "The crowd is huge."

It also proves hugely responsive as Harding, speaking vigorously from the rear platform of *The Superb,* hits his stride, as usual dispensing with the microphone. Mencken, listening along with a dozen or so other reporters sprinkled throughout the crowd, discerns that Harding has begun to develop deeper, edgier, more complex themes, all the while his language has grown simpler.

"How can we permit a group of Americans," asks Harding, "Americans as numerous as the entire population of some European nations—to remain walled off in their own land, simply because of the color of their skin? Not only does this isolate and demean *them*, it denies this country their rich contribution. It is short-sighted. It is grievously un-American. It is wrong."

Back in Washington, Lodge, flanked by Paxton and Guthrie, has launched a round-robin counter-offensive, matching Harding, speech for speech, point for point. Two hours after Harding's attack on segregation reaches Washington, his three former colleagues are holding a press conference on the Senate steps, facing reporters from within the bosom of a small, carefully chosen audience of true believers.

"God Almighty has fixed boundaries between the races," insists Lodge, "and not even a President of the United States can improve upon the Creator's work."

As *The Superb* makes its way further west, Harding finds himself addressing ever larger and more demonstrative crowds, indoors or out, and in every kind of weather. The pace is exhausting, but bonding with increasing numbers of "The People" serves to revitalize his delivery.

In Salt Lake City:

"All the great naval powers are now inspired by America's selfless example. . . "

From Washington, Lodge fires back:

"In five months this profligate, naive president has sent more worthy ships to the bottom than all the admirals of the world have sunk in five centuries."

Harding in Casper:

"We need to build more schools and fewer jails, produce more books and fewer bullets. . . "

Committee, Oscar Keller presiding, glare down from an elevated dais at Harry Daugherty, seated at the witness table, smoothly fielding questions. Behind him, the hearing room is packed.

Keller is getting nowhere. "Have you any idea, Mr. Attorney General, how securities in a German munitions firm in negotiations with the government found their way to a bank owned by your brother?"

"To quote the Bible, Mr. Chairman—," begins Daugherty, prompting Congressman Weeks to mutter to Congressman Fish, "May God strike him dead."

"—I am not my brother's keeper," continues Daugherty. "How my brother chose to run his bank is entirely his affair."

"Your brother," Keller asserts, "apparently chose to run his bank into the ground, taking thousands of depositors with him."

"Most regrettable, most regrettable. But as I say. . . "

Keller cuts him off. "If I may, sir —" Congressman Hayes in the seat adjacent slips Keller a document. "How is it," continues Keller, referring to Hayes' note, "that a cigar maker who prior to Prohibition used an average of 480 gallons of alcohol to process tobacco, last year received permission from your office to draw 520,000 gallons? That's enough booze to. . . "

Across the road, just outside the Senate building, Roxie Forbes pulls her Cord convertible into a center stall of a restricted parking zone as if it had been explicitly set aside for her. She flounces out. Overhead, the capital's mid-August sun blazes vindictively, but Roxie wears evening makeup and a mink jacket.

Thanks to a subpoena from Walsh, the Wheeler Committee finally has itself a witness who is eager to perform. Half-draped over the witness table, occasionally taking a drag from her pearl cigarette-holder, Roxie leaps at Walsh's uncharacteristically sympathetic questions. "I'm not sure where my husband is, sir. Gay Parie, last time I heard, living up a storm." She dabs a tear with her silk green and purple handkerchief. "Leaves me stuck here. In dire poverty."

"I'm sorry, Mrs. Forbes," says Walsh. "It must be very difficult for you. . . "

"All I did was marry the man. My one mistake. Now I'm left in the lurch with just a car, this old coat, and every creditor in Washington hounding me!"

While Roxie turns on the tears for the Senate, in the House, Congressman Hayes is turning up the heat on Daugherty. "Did you not summarily reassign the attorney handling the prosecution to Guam, just before trial was to commence?"

Daugherty shakes his head. "Uh, I have no specific details on that case. Generally we send our attorneys wherever they are most needed at a particular time. . . "

"Can you at least tell this committee, however approximately, the number of war profiteers your office has actually sent to prison? A hundred? Twenty? Five? Two?"

"Sorry, sir, not off the top of my head. Congressman Hayes, you must understand, the federal courts are crowded. . . "

By contrast, Roxie Forbes seems able to recall precise details for Walsh at every turn. "That month—July of '22 we're talking about—Charlie received enough champagne to fill our swimming pool."

"Any idea who sent it?" asks Walsh.

"Yeah. Out in California, Charlie had the V.A. build this hospital for alcoholic veterans. Right in the middle of a vineyard, if you can believe that. Some little old winemaker must have been real appreciative." Roxie leans forward. The committeemen study her intently. Scores of state secrets might well be hidden in her cleavage. "Then there were those suitcases of cash. Tell the truth, I never in my life seen a thousand dollar bill—till I hitched up with Charlie. Haven't seen none since, either. Right now I'd settle for a ten spot. . . "

Congressman Hayes keeps the pressure on Daugherty. "Please just answer the question, Mr. Attorney General. It was really quite simple and straightforward. How many . . . ?"

"I'm not able to tell you at this time, Congressman."

"What is your present relationship to one Jess Smith—offices at—1625 K Street? Could you just possibly tell us that, sir?"

No answer.

"That's *Smith* Mr. Daugherty. Jess Smith."

Congressman Weeks mutters to Congressman Fish. "Rat's in a corner now."

"He's an old rat," replies Fish. "Lotsa holes to run to."

Finally, Daugherty responds. "I decline to answer, sir."

"On what conceivable grounds?" demands Congressman Keller.

"National security, Mr. Chairman—and to protect the integrity of the office of the Attorney General—and to protect the President."

The ceiling falls in. Keller hits the gavel and shouts over the roar of voices. "All right! Quiet! *Quiet*!"

To no avail.

40.

The mail is blessedly slow to Alaska, and the territorial press largely indifferent to events in faraway Washington, thereby giving Harding about a half-week's respite from the growing avalanche of bad news. But homeward bound, the presidential yacht is still a good day from its destination of Seattle when just before dinner, a U.S. Navy seaplane catches up, cuts across the sunset and lands alongside. Harding watches gloomily from his cabin window as the cargo door behind a wing drops open. Two marines scurry out to the edge of the yacht's deck, extend a pole to the seaplane and hook a leather pouch marked with the presidential seal. Harding sighs and shakes his head as the pouch is hoisted aboard.

The 10:00 P.M bells find Harding on deck, alone, pacing in a circle. Since departing Alaska he's developed a cough, and every so often, pauses to lean on the railing and clear his lungs. Then, too restless to stop for more than a few seconds, he returns to his pacing.

Harding's butler appears. "Er, excuse me, Mr. President."

"Ah, yes, Dirkson."

"Just wondering if there's anything more. . . "

"You should have turned in hours ago. I'm fine. You have a good night."

"Yes, sir. Good night, Mr. President." He turns to leave.

"Dirkson, may I ask—who'd you vote for in the last election?"

"Well I wanted to vote for you, Mr. President."

"Wanted to?"

"Oh yes, sir. Seemed clear to me you were the best man."

"But—but you didn't."

"When I got down to the voting booth they said I didn't

pass the lit-ra-cy test. I thought I'd done pretty well, but that's what the man said." Dirkson pauses. "He was a white man."

"I see. I'm sorry, Dirkson."

"Sure glad you got in anyway, Mr. President."

"Mm. Then—I haven't let you down."

"Oh no, *sir*, Mr. President. Not one bit."

"Well. . . thank you, Dirkson. Appreciate it. Good night."

"Good night, sir."

He leaves. Moments later, Harding has a paroxysm of coughing.

On the foredeck, Sawyer hears the cough and follows it to its source. "Don't like the sound of that, Warren."

"Well, yer up late, Doc," Harding replies, as he recovers his breath.

"Never mind me. Shouldn't *you* be trying to get some rest? I understand tomorrow's a big one."

"Can't sleep. Not even with those phenobarbs."

"Worse than on the train."

Harding nods, leans on the railing, and looks out into the darkness.

"No square wheels on the boat," observes Sawyer.

"No. No square wheels." Harding is silent for a long moment. Then he straightens up decisively and turns to Sawyer. "I've made up my mind. I'm going to order Albert Fall to resign. I've wired him to meet us in San Francisco next week. I want to tell the sonofabitch face to face."

"He ought to have had the grace to quit weeks ago."

"Yeah. Seems he's still insisting he's done nothing wrong." He sighs deeply. "My enemies I can handle, Doc. It's my friends, my goddamn friends —!"

He begins to cough again, greatly alarming Sawyer. "Let me get those pills. . . "

"No, I'm okay. It's all this damn fresh air." Harding recaptures his wind, and sits down tentatively at the end of a deck chair. "Al's not the worst of it, Doc. Not by a long shot." He takes a breath and lets it out slowly. "Received some transcripts—flown in this evening. . . Christ, I'm so tired. Wish I could sleep. Just go to sleep. . . " Another cough.

"It's awfully chilly out here, Warren. You really should come inside."

Harding shakes his head. "I feel trapped in that itty-bitty cabin." He slides back and settles into the deck chair. "Let me have that blanket, will you, Doc? See if I can't catch a few winks. Right here." He shakes his head. "You know, I've always thought, if you accommodated people, showed them every possible kindness, things would work out. That's what I believed. All my life. Pathetic . . . "

He closes his eyes.

The darkened corridor of the senatorial office building is otherwise deserted as a pair of gloved hands artfully pick the lock of a door titled *SEN. FRANCIS WALSH*. The door swings open and the janitor from the *Baltimore Sun* enters, flips on a flashlight and begins rifling the files. Then he turns to the senator's safe.

There is late-night activity in an office on K Street as well. Jess, in a marginally controlled panic, is feeding papers and ledgers into the fireplace as fast as the flames will consume them.

The phone rings.

Jess picks up. Hears nothing. "Yeah?" He listens. "Hello?" A click at the other end, then a dial tone. Jess slams down the receiver and dumps everything remaining into the fire, all in a heap.

Moments later, he sails out the front door, rushes down the steps, and hurriedly begins across the road to his car, parked several spaces ahead of a yellow Stutz roadster. It is nearly 4:00 A.M., and K Street is as quiet as death.

Suddenly Jess is startled by the sound of galloping hooves as a driverless horse-drawn *Purity Milk* wagon shoots out of the darkness and bears down on him. He tries scrambling back on the curb but the frightened horse, blinders on, seems to swerve straight for him. A flying hoof wallops Jess in the head. The wagon jumps the curb, crushing Jess'chest under a wheel, then tilts over, careening against the iron fence of the K Street house, milk bottles scattering and smashing everywhere. The horse, broken free of its harness, gallops on down the street.

Once again, all is quiet.

Jess lies face up in a puddle of milk, a small concentric pool of blood oozing from his scalp. His broken wrist lies at an odd angle across his sightless eyes, wristwatch still ticking. Timex.

41.

Harding, looking especially grim, Florence, Hoover, Sawyer, and Special Counsel Travis, huddle together in a Packard limousine as it speeds through sparse midday traffic towards Seattle's coliseum. A Secret Serviceman covers each running board.

"Some sort of freak accident," Travis explains. "A runaway milk wagon. . . "

"I can't believe it," says Harding, shaking his head. "A goddamn milk wagon! Everything's going to hell. By God, when I get back to Washington. . . !" A cough cuts him short. Subsiding, he turns to Travis. "Hear from the Attorney General yet?"

"No, Mr. President," says Travis, "we've still not been able to reach him."

"I'll bet we're not the only ones," growls Sawyer.

Mencken watches with the rest of the press corps from behind a velvet rope as a haggard and winded Harding, his entourage, and its Secret Service guardians, together negotiate the coliseum's front steps, today a thicket of little American flags and clusters of cheering, waving citizens, barely held in check by a thin line of uniformed police.

A reporter from the *Seattle Herald* turns to Mencken. "Christ, he looks like death warmed over."

"Yeah," sighs Mencken. "This is a strange country when it comes to Presidents. Practically worship them, for openers. Expect them to perform miracles. Then when they can't, we kill 'em."

The presidential party reaches the entranceway. Harding pauses to catch his breath. The crowd, pressing good-naturedly against the police restraints, is warm, enthusiastic, and supportive.

But there are dissenters. "When you gonna clean house, Warren?" shouts one.

"You tell a man by the company he keeps," adds another.

A third asks loudly: "Where's the government auction this week, Mr. President—the Lincoln bedroom?"

The surrounding crowd jostles and shushes the three dissidents, but Harding's heard them well enough; their words continue to sting like a slap in the face as he and his small group continue inside.

The coliseum, packed past capacity, waits eagerly as Harding, perceptibly shaky only to those in the front rows, mounts the mike-studded podium. Hoover, Hughes and Florence take their seats on stage just behind him.

Harding's arrival at the bank of microphones elicits thunderous applause and brings the crowd to its feet. After a few moments, he holds up his hands for quiet. The audience keeps clapping. Harding smiles and waits, discreetly coughing once into his hand.

In living rooms across America—urban, suburban and rural—families large and small bunch around their Philco's and Stromberg-Carlsons, listening along with the President to the applause. Nan too, sits by the radio in her Washington apartment, awaiting the sound of Harding's voice. Her pulse quickens as she hears him say, "My fellow Americans—."

The applause finally dies away, the audience settles expectantly in their seats, and Harding, the seventh draft of his speech in hand, begins, his voice strained.

"Every President strives, however imperfectly, to pick the best possible people to help him do his job. You'd be quite amazed, I think, at the enormous number of worthy folk knocking on his door, all hoping for a government job. I never knew how many Hardings there were in the United States, or how many distant cousins I had. Till I got elected."

Laughter from the audience.

"Seems every one of them is available for public service."

More laughter. Harding coughs a little, then continues.

"I'm happy to report that up in Alaska I caught a bit of a cold. At last I have something I can give to everybody."

That brings down the house.

After a few moments, Harding holds up a hand. When the laughter and applause finally subside, his tone has changed, and his voice has recaptured some of its old resonance. "The federal government is enormous, as you know. And with so many posts to be filled, from time to time the wrong person gets appointed." He pauses. "Sorry to say, we've all been hearing some serious accusations leveled against certain prominent White House officials."

Several of those listening in back of the main floor and in far corners of the balcony cup their ears.

"I must tell you, no one's been more distressed by this than your President. After all, I'm the one who gave them their jobs. Well I promise: in short order we'll have the charges sorted out. Fact distinguished from allegation. Then we'll kick any rotten apples right onto the street. I plan to do it personally. My foot." He points. "This one right here."

Even seasoned members of the press are applauding and laughing now. A reporter from the *Saturday Evening Post* wonders out loud, "Who the hell's writing his stuff?"

"I think he is," replies Mencken.

Harding's countenance darkens. "But I dare say, some of what you've had to listen to 'bout *me* has been even rougher. Downright nasty. Courtesy of a few old Senate colleagues of mine."

In her Washington apartment, Nan puts down her knitting. Never in a public speech has she heard Harding speak so personally.

"Listen to these noxious naysayers," continues Harding, "and you start to get the idea that my proposals for a better world are ill-conceived. Poisonous. A real bad deal for America. Well, if you will allow, here's what your President believes to be a real bad deal."

Harding pauses. The audience falls absolutely still.

"It's when rival nations compete in costly, escalating preparation for each other's destruction. When, on a planet of some six hundred million souls, some eighty-nine quarrelsome countries, there's no impartial world court to which they might turn so as to settle disputes—no international 'justice of the peace' to help decide who's right and who's wrong—short of war. It's when. . . it's when. . . "

Harding cannot catch his breath. Ashen-faced, he drops his speech—the papers flutter to the floor just by Hoover's feet. Harding grabs the lectern for support, a crushing pain in his chest.

In Washington, Nan is puzzled by the silence.

Hoover scoops the sheets up and hurries over to Harding. "Mr. President. . . !"

Harding's spasm passes. He reaches for the speech, and whispers, "I'm okay, thank you, Herbert. Should never have eaten both those crabs last night."

"Will you be. . . ?"

Harding nods. An intensely apprehensive Hoover returns to his seat, but manages a nod and smile for Florence.

Harding thumbs through the pages in his hands—they're out of order, a few sheets upside down. Doesn't matter. He lays them on the lectern and continues extemporaneously.

"A bad deal, for you, for me, for America, is one where might makes right. Where an entire people may be declared an enemy simply because they have a different language, a different religion, a different bit of pigment in their skin. Where there festers an unbridgeable chasm between the lives of the rich and those of the poor."

Each one of his listeners—white, black, Hispanic, Asian—hang on his every word.

"The world has been thus for a long time. It is not likely to quickly change its ways. But *this* administration, the *Harding* administration, believes that America, over time, can make a difference. That we can build a land where the strong are just and the weak are secure, a land where the less fortunate cast off their chains of poverty. This President knows, deep down, that a government pure of heart can enable us to do together what would be impossible for any of us, however dedicated, to do alone. Working hand in hand, you and I in partnership—the good Lord willing—we shall make this oft-battered world happier, safer, a better place for our children. Together, we shall strive to guarantee a fruitful life—for all mankind."

Harding gazes from row to row. Each member of the audience feels as if he's looking directly at him. "*That,* my good friends, is my heart's desire."

In her apartment, Nan, eyes moist, listens open-mouthed at this echo of her own very words.

"I thank you all," concludes Harding, "and God bless."

For a moment time stops. The audience, enveloped by Harding's almost painful sincerity, sits in a reverent silence. And then ringing applause and cheers erupt from every corner of the assembly hall and spill from radio sets across the country and on out into Nan's living room as she shares in her President's triumph, tears streaming down her cheeks.

In the dressing room nearest the coliseum's stage, Florence anxiously holds her husband's hand as he sags back in a wooden chair, shirt off, Sawyer's stethoscope up against his chest. Continuing applause and shouts of "Harding, Harding" leak through the chamber's thin walls.

"I dunno, Warren —," says Sawyer as he lifts the stethoscope out of his ears. "It's possible you had a heart seizure. A little one."

"That was a heck of a big crab last night. . . "

"We really should bring in a specialist. . . "

"I feel fine," Harding insists. He starts to cough again.

"Yeah," says Sawyer, "that would make you a great epitaph. 'He felt fine.'"

"I do."

"You feel like hell. Florence —?"

"Wurr'n. Let's do as Doc says."

Harding sighs. "Why now? Why does it have to happen now?" He tries to rise, feels dizzy, and flops back in the chair, terrifically short of breath, his face shining with sweat.

"Stay put!" orders Sawyer. "Till we get a cardiologist."

"Right. You're the doctor," says Harding weakly.

42.

Nan, now distinctly pregnant, is amongst the theatergoers spilling out from The Biograph's matinee. Afternoon newspapers have just hit the stands, the paperboys touting headlines about the President's attack to passersby. Copies are snatched up as fast as the boys can collect their nickels. Nan rises to the challenge, securing several copies each of the *Post*, the *Star*, and the *Bulletin*.

That afternoon, worrisome news came that my poor Warren was suddenly indisposed. From eating some bad crab. The doctors asked that he cancel all appearances for the rest of the week. Go straight through to San Francisco to convalesce. I'd been keeping close count of his speeches—one hundred thirty-five in fifty-two days—and remember thinking: Well, at least he'll finally get a little rest, thank God. At the time I had no inkling—I guess nobody did—just how ill my darling really was.

A classically fine San Francisco summer afternoon—foggy and bitterly cold. The Pierce-Arrow carrying Harding, Florence, Hoover, Sawyer and Travis, encircled by a motorcycle escort, makes its stately way to the Palace Hotel. Outside its Market Street entrance, a small crowd awaits. It includes a quiet line of black men and women carrying signs:

EQUAL PAY FOR EQUAL WORK
and
ALL MEN ARE CREATED EQUAL
and
COLORED PEOPLE HAVE RIGHTS TOO

The limousine glides on past the front hotel entrance and around the corner to a side door. Harding peers through his window at the demonstrators. He is wrapped neck to toe in a blanket, his hair entirely white much like Woodrow

Wilson's just three years before. He coughs. Then he asks, "What the hell's going on out there, Mr. Travis?"

"Seems some Coloreds are putting on a public display, sir. They're demanding equal rights."

"*Demanding?*" asks Harding. "Where do they get such ideas?"

"I believe from you, Mr. President."

Seven thousand miles due east across a continent and an ocean, dawn gently lightens the sky over Paris. Charlie Forbes, entirely alone on the highest deck of the Eiffel Tower, finishes a last cigarette, carefully removes his spectacles, and slips them into his breast pocket. Then he climbs over the rail and heads rapidly for the concourse 984 feet below.

43.

That evening, propped up in the bed of the Palace's presidential suite, Harding enjoys a game of poker with Sawyer, who sits alongside. He looks and feels considerably better.

The flower-filled room is further cluttered with bundles of letters and cards. Florence is at the desk, wading through a stack. Harding glances up from his hand—a full house, as yet unbeknownst to Sawyer—and turns to his wife. "You can't possibly respond to them all, Duchess."

"I intend to make a good start. Listen to this poem: 'From Tommy B. Lawton, age 10. *We love all our Presidents but the best are so few—Washington, Lincoln, McKinley and you.*'"

"McKinley?" asks Sawyer, "Why McKinley? What a dud. Only thing he did of note was get himself assassinated."

The old newspaper editor in Harding slips out. "Our young poet probably liked the rhythm: 'Mc*Kin*ley and *you.*'" He smiles, a faraway look in his eyes. "Back in Marion, remember? The *Star* used to publish a 'Poem of the Week.' I recall, there was this little girl who had written one. Sweet, passionate, straight from her heart . . . "

The phone on the desk rings.

Florence sighs. "I'm gonna have a word with that switchboard." She picks up. "Hello?" She listens, then turns to her husband. "Mr. Hoover and Mr. Hughes wonder if you're up to a brief conference."

"Of course, of course." A cough, but a small one. Then he collects Sawyer's money.

Florence looks at Sawyer, who nods. She turns back to the phone. "Doc Sawyer says only a few minutes." She listens. "All right."

"Good," says Harding. "Some things I want to run past them. For tomorrow's speech. And we should decide the best way to deal with my other distinguished cabinet member. Albert Fall should be here tonight, Daugherty by tomorrow."

"I have it. How about a double lynching?" suggests Sawyer. "Two on a rope. Save the taxpayers some money." There's a knock on the door. Sawyer goes to open it. "I'll even furnish the rope. But I *don't* think you're quite up to making any speeches yet, Warren. You heard the heart men. They all say ten days bed rest. Minimum."

Hoover and Hughes enter. Hoover carries a small file, Hughes a handful of newspapers. Harding is almost his old, cheerful self. "Come in, gentlemen, come on in."

It's shortly before midnight in Washington. Nan, wearing a nightgown and slippers, replaces the receiver of her bedside candlestick phone, pads over to the bathroom, retrieves a glass of water, returns to set it on her nightstand, then turns down the bed covers.

That evening the news from California was encouraging. Reports were that the President's illness had broken, and that he would soon resume his speaking engagements.

She climbs into bed and opens a book entitled *"Preparatory Schools of England."*

I took a chance, called long distance, tried to get a cheery message to him through Dr. Sawyer.

But the operator said all lines were jammed. I wish to God I'd kept trying. I wish to God. . .

It's the end of a long day for the President and his group. Sawyer and Hughes have already left the suite for their own quarters; Hoover too is finally headed for the door. There he pauses, nods at Florence, and turns back for a moment to face Harding, resting comfortably in bed. "Don't let the stories out of Washington get to you, Mr. President. You make the best possible appointments you can with what you know at the time. Politics often comes down to a choice between greater and lesser evils."

Harding sighs and shakes his head. "Yes, Herbert. But how do you tell which is which?"

In Washington, Nan has fallen asleep, the book still in her hands.

Nine-fifteen P.M in San Francisco, close to the Hardings' old bedtime back in Marion, Ohio. They are finally alone, Florence reading aloud from the local newspapers, Harding listening from the bed, sitting up, his back supported by a mountain of pillows. Though his breathing is shallow, he remains attentive.

Florence puts the *Chronicle* aside and picks up the *Examiner*. "Now, my word, listen to this: 'The President has broken totally with the old guard of his own party. He has laid out a hopeful, and in some ways, a brilliant new pathway for the country—indeed, for the world. His personal reputation has never been higher.'" She looks at him. He nods and smiles in satisfaction. She reads further. "'His last reception, in Seattle earlier this week, was stupendous and well deserved.'"

Harding listens but is having trouble breathing again.

Florence continues. "'The public thus far appears unimpressed by rumors of serious impropriety involving members of his administration, none of which, it must be emphasized, directly implicate the President himself.'" She looks over at him. "You see? All of your worrying. For nothing."

Harding gasps and stops breathing. He stares at her, glassy-eyed, then slumps back.

"Wurr'n!" She rushes to him. "Wurr'n, oh dear God, Wurr'n!"

In her Washington bedroom, Nan suddenly sits bolt upright in bed, wide-eyed, sweat streaming from her face.

44.

Two days later, Nan looks past tears and through her veil as the presidential funeral procession lumbers towards the train terminal at the end of Market Street, where *The Superb* waits, now draped in black crepe. Her gloved hand offers up a solemn little wave as Harding's coffin passes just a few feet in front of her.

Watching you move slowly by, I thought of you lying there, all alone. How turbulent your life had been these past few years, how restless and despairing you had become towards the end. And then, suddenly you were gone, and there was nothing more for me to do. It was over. How could that be? It felt to me as if we our lives together, as if you and I, were just beginning.

Washington would be no place for me now. Not without you. It was time to return home. Time to take our unborn child far from that soulless city of illusion and its treacheries. Back to Marion, Ohio, where one might grow up amidst the virtues of simple honesty and integrity that you embodied, and which so endeared you to all America.

I will do my best to uphold your ideals. I will honor you in my motherhood and my maturity. I will make you proud of me and of our child.

Be at peace, my dear Mr. President.

EPILOGUE

Marion, Ohio, April 18th, 1930.

Two squirrels scamper up and across an alabaster dome supported by twenty-three marble Corinthian columns. One chases the other down the foremost column to a gravelly clearing in front of the sun-burnished edifice, where some two hundred people sit on folding chairs, watching as a somber President Herbert Hoover mounts the podium.

A small Marine brass band is off to the side, finishing a dirge. The last strains slowly die away over the President's crypt.

Well, it took them seven years to complete my mausoleum—the "Harding Memorial," as they like to call her now. Most deceased Presidents get properly interred within a few months of their kicking off. But not me. What with yet another scandal uncovered almost every week, you can bet contributions dried up pretty darn quick, and Italian marble don't come cheap. People felt sorry for me at first, then decided it was probably my fault after all. And I guess, much of it was. I was the guy in charge. So for the longest time I just lay here under some scaffolding and a pile of stones. Then when they finally get the damn thing up, Old Pickle-Face, President Coolidge, refuses to come anywhere near it. Wasn't till Herbert got elected that we had a President with the balls to come put in a good word for me.

Hoover begins the dedication.

"Ten years ago, Warren Harding was elected as an image, a lovely, artfully tinted portrait of the sort of man we might all picture as our President—infinitely wise, statesmanlike, with the will, intelligence and talent to do the world enormous good. It was a romantic American fiction as Warren Harding, *the man*, entered the White House. But by the time of his death, *President* Harding had somehow managed to grow into that image, making it a reality. Warren Harding recreated himself and was, perhaps, on the edge of greatness."

*I'm not so sure about **that**, but thank you, Herbert.*

Hoover pauses and lets his eyes sweep over the faces of the mourners, among them H. L. Mencken; Everett Sawyer, Jr., M.D., on behalf of his late father; and Carrie Phillips, at fifty-eight a most handsome woman, seated with her second—and far younger—husband by her side.

Hoover continues. "It was his tragedy that at the very moment of triumph, as he struggled so mightily toward perfection, he was betrayed by friends to whom, in old misjudgments, he had given his trust. In the end they broke his heart. But whatever the mis-steps of Warren Harding—the all too mortal man—we today salute Warren Harding, the gallant, imperishable President. And we honor his extraordinary strength and courage."

Hoover had thought to speak longer, but flooded with emotions, now finds that he can go no further. Slowly he steps down. A bugler begins playing Taps.

Whew! What can I possibly say after all that? Fine fellow, Herbert Hoover. Real shame he's the one stuck with cleaning up the mess Coolidge and I left behind.

The crowd starts to disperse.

*And **what** a mess. Poor Charlie Forbes goes and jumps off the goddamn Eiffel Tower. Jess Smith probably murdered. Al Fall sent to prison for accepting a bribe Sinclair is acquitted of having given him. Daugherty's neck saved by a hung jury Burns is convicted of having bribed. The economy in shambles. Wall Street twelve feet under. And on and on.*

Most of the crowd has left. The musicians, all packed up, file off the bandstand.

And my new will, providing for Nan and the little one? Disappears, along with many of my personal papers. The Duchess' delicate hand, I'll bet, rest her soul.

The memorial is deserted now but for two—Nan Britton, eyes shining, and her seven-year-old daughter, Elizabeth Ann.

Ah—doesn't much matter any more, I s'pose. Already most folks have forgotten. Who the hell is Warren Harding, they ask. Except you, dearest Nan. You'll not forget me, will you. And I know, no matter what they say about me, you'll always care. For you know the truth.

Mother and daughter take one last look up at the memorial, then turn and hand in hand, slowly walk away.

Goodbye, my true and deepest love. Try not to be too sad. And goodbye, precious child.

Elizabeth Ann cocks her head and turns back around as if she's actually heard her father's farewell. She tugs on her mother's arm. Nan stops and points to the rustling leaves of a nearby tree. Then they resume their steps, but the child's not convinced. She *knows* what she heard.

Lovely little girl, don't you think? Looks just like her dad.

Harding's daughter glances behind her once again and breaks out into a half smile.

In 1931 Nan Britton wrote and, after difficulty with censors, published a best-seller, "THE PRESIDENT'S DAUGHTER," telling about her life with Warren Harding. Portraying him as the honest and compassionate man she knew him to be, Nan did her best to salvage his reputation from posterity's disrepute. She used her substantial royalties to open the Elizabeth Ann Home for unwed mothers.

Her book includes quotations from several of Harding's speeches, including this from one given in Minneapolis on July 21st, 1923, shortly before his death:

"Ask not what your country can do for you; Ask—what may I do for my country?"

According to a brief, little noticed obituary in the Marion Daily Star, Nan Britton died on August 23rd, 1993, at the age of 96, seventy years to the day of the death of her beloved president.